"Do you like bourbon now. Bourbon or water. Or bourbon and water."

"It's fine," she said. When Zane picked up the bottle and poured them each about two fingers' worth of the amber liquid, she accepted the glass.

"I didn't know you were a bourbon drinker."

She wasn't. She didn't drink much, and the strong taste of bourbon wasn't her favorite, but tonight it would do.

"There's a lot you don't know about me."

This time his right brow arched. A challenge. He didn't quite smile, but his eyes lingered on hers long enough to be suggestive. He made a *harrumph* noise that seemed as if he was considering the possibility of them or sizing her up. It was thrilling and frightening, electric and grounding.

Flirting with Zane was like a wild roller-coaster ride that twisted her every which way. Sometimes it made her feel as if she was about to tumble out of herself, or shoot straight off the edge of the universe. But when the car that was his attention finally delivered her to the station with a buzzing rush, she was always well aware she'd never been in any real danger of falling. Scratch that—she'd *fallen* a long time ago...

CELEBRATION, TX:
Love is just a celebration away...

Dear Reader,

I love hearing stories about how couples met. Whether it was love at first sight or a slow-burning ember that took its time to spark, I love learning how two people found their way to each other.

Lucy Campbell and Zane Phillips, the hero and heroine of *A Bride, a Barn, and a Baby*, took the long way around the barn...er...the long way to falling in love. Lucy, the eternal romantic, was in love with him for as far back as she can remember, but it took a while for Zane to realize the love he needed had been right in front of him all along.

I hope you enjoy Lucy and Zane's story as much as I enjoyed writing it. Please join me on Facebook at Facebook.com/nrobardsthompson, on Instagram at Instagram.com/nancyrthompson, on Twitter at Twitter.com/nrtwrites or drop me a line at nrobardsthompson@yahoo.com. I love to hear from readers!

Warmly,

Nancy

A Bride, a Barn, and a Baby

Nancy Robards Thompson

HARLEQUIN® SPECIAL EDITION®

PLEASE RECYCLE • THIS PRODUCT IS RECYCLABLE

Recycling programs
for this product may
not exist in your area.

ISBN-13: 978-0-373-62359-4

A Bride, a Barn, and a Baby

Copyright © 2017 by Nancy Robards Thompson

HARLEQUIN®
www.Harlequin.com

Printed in U.S.A.

National bestselling author **Nancy Robards Thompson** holds a degree in journalism. She worked as a newspaper reporter until she realized reporting "just the facts" bored her silly. Now that she has much more content to report to her muse, Nancy loves writing women's fiction and romance full-time. Critics have deemed her work "funny, smart and observant." She resides in Florida with her husband and daughter. You can reach her at nancyrobardsthompson.com and Facebook.com/nancyrobardsthompsonbooks.

Books by Nancy Robards Thompson

Harlequin Special Edition

Celebration, TX

The Cowboy's Runaway Bride

Celebrations, Inc.

His Texas Christmas Bride
How to Marry a Doctor
A Celebration Christmas
Celebration's Baby
Celebration's Family
Celebration's Bride
Texas Christmas
Texas Magic
Texas Wedding

The Fortunes of Texas: The Secret Fortunes

Fortune's Surprise Engagement

The Fortunes of Texas: Welcome to Horseback Hollow

Falling for Fortune

The Fortunes of Texas: Whirlwind Romance

Fortune's Unexpected Groom

Visit the Author Profile page
at Harlequin.com for more titles.

This book is dedicated to Kathleen O'Brien
for your friendship and spot-on plotting advice.

Chapter One

May 2017

"I know I should've called first," Lucy Campbell said when Zane Phillips opened his front door, "but I come bearing gifts."

Standing in the doorway, looking cranky, his big frame taking up a lot of space, Zane silently eyed her offerings.

"I brought *The Breakfast Club*, *Pretty in Pink*, *St. Elmo's Fire* and *Say Anything...* and a few others." She handed the DVDs to him one by one as she read off each title. He frowned as he looked at them, and then he held up the one on top.

"This is a problem," he said, looking at the movie

as if he didn't know what to do with it. "I'm not in the mood to *say anything*."

"That's why I brought over a selection." Lucy reached into his personal space and tapped the DVD case. "If you're not in the mood for that movie, you can choose another one."

He shook his head. "No. Luce, you're not understanding me. I'm not in the mood for talking. Period. I don't feel like company tonight."

"I understand you better than you think I do. Hence the movies." And the reason she hadn't called before showing up. "You don't have to talk. All you have to do is watch. And eat Chinese food."

She held up a brown paper sack.

"Are you going to let me in? The kung pao beef is getting cold."

Storm clouds were rolling in and the fragrance of rain hung in the humid air.

"You brought kung pao?" His tone was lighter.

She nodded. "And General Tso's chicken, fried rice and egg rolls."

She'd known it wouldn't be easy getting past his front door. That was why she'd brought the food. She thrust the large brown sack at him, and he almost dropped the stack of movies. He shifted the DVDs into one hand and accepted the bag. Pushing past him, Lucy stepped onto the beige carpet into the living room of Zane's Bridgemont Farms house and squinted into the dim light. The curtains were drawn. The only light on was the one in the kitchen.

It cast enough of a golden glow to illuminate the mess in the front room. An empty pizza box, spent beer cans, a couple pairs of socks, some wadded-up jeans and a pair of mud-caked boots lying askew on the carpet. It all looked as if he had left it where he had dropped it, amid the stacks of cardboard boxes and piles of things he'd been sorting.

"Sorry about the mess," he mumbled as he grabbed up the jeans and socks and kicked the boots into a corner. A guy's way of cleaning. Her brother Ethan had similar tactics before Chelsea came into his life. Now, thanks to his future wife, Ethan was not only in love, but his house was also spotless.

"I'm still trying to figure out what to do with Mom's things. I've been bringing over a few boxes at a time. There's still so much stuff in her house— er, your family's house."

"You know there's no hurry to move her things out," Lucy said. "We don't have renters. You can take as long as you need. You don't have to bring everything over here to sort it if you don't have room for it. Just leave it at the house."

"Bossy." He scowled. "I've got a system. It's working fine."

For decades, his mom, Dorothy, had rented the small bungalow on the lower edge of the Campbells' property. Zane and his brother, Ian, had grown up there with their mother, who'd stayed in the house long after her boys had moved out and moved on with their lives. Lucy thought she and her brothers had made it clear that Zane could take all the time he needed to get Dorothy's things in order before he turned over the keys. That was how people treated each other in Celebration—they compromised and met each other halfway, especially in the wake of a family crisis. And Dorothy Phillips's surrender to an aggressive form of lymphoma that had ended her life nearly as fast as the disease had appeared hadn't been just a family crisis—it was a loss felt by the entire town. Many friends and neighbors, including Lucy, had reached out and offered to help Zane with the move out, but true to his lone-wolf ways, Zane had politely turned down the gestures of goodwill in favor of going it alone. He said he needed time to think, time to figure out what to do with the remnants of his mother's life. Everyone had respected his wishes and left him alone. Well, everyone except for Lucy. She knew him well enough to understand that sometimes Zane's pride kept him from asking for or accepting help. Sometimes Zane needed to be shown that his way wasn't always the best way. Tonight was a case in point.

"Why don't you take your *system* into the kitchen and get us some plates?" Lucy said. "I'll get the first DVD queued up and ready to play."

"The *first* one? You're not planning on watching all of them, are you?"

"Of course we are, that's why I brought them."

"You'll be here all night."

Lucy smiled and cocked a brow in the most suggestive way possible.

He shook his head. "Don't start with me, Campbell." He handed her the movies and grabbed a trio of beer cans off the coffee table to clear a spot for the sack of food. She watched him disappear around the corner into the kitchen, where he rattled around for a few minutes. It sounded like he was tidying up in there, too.

Lucy turned on a table lamp. In the light's golden glow, she could see that the place wasn't dirty as much as it was cluttered boxes of Dorothy's things. What with juggling the funeral arrangements, moving his mom's possessions to his house and his job as general manager of Bridgemont Farms, his living room looked rougher around the edges than usual. Then again, it didn't take much to make such a small house look messy.

A stack of boxes lined the far wall. Several small piles consisting of various household appliances and articles of clothing, shoes and accessories sat waiting on the floor. A couple of garbage bags sagged in the corner, probably filled with items that hadn't made the cut.

Ian had come back to Celebration for the funeral. He'd done what he could to help clear out the house while he was here, but Zane had mentioned that sifting through more than a quarter century's worth of their mother's life had proved too arduous a task in the days immediately after the funeral. They hadn't even made a dent before Ian had had to leave and get back to his job in Colorado. That left Zane to finish the job and tie up all the loose ends.

As Lucy picked up the empty pizza box and started to put it in one of the garbage bags, she spied Dorothy's sketchbook in the trash. She set aside the box and took out the book, running her hand over its tattered and faded no-frills cover before she leafed through the pages of hand-drawn fashion illustrations.

Lucy's heart clenched. In her mind's eye she could see Dorothy sitting on the house's back porch at the patio table with a cigarette and a cup of coffee, drawing in this book. Lucy used to love to watch her. Dorothy had patiently answered Lucy's never-ending stream of little-girl questions as the woman's deft hands brought to life the magical vignettes. After Dorothy had made Lucy's prom dress, Lucy had always thought of her as her very own fairy godmother.

Why would Zane throw this away? Lucy started to call to him in the kitchen, but it dawned on her that if he'd tossed such a personal item, it had to mean that in this moment it was too painful for him to keep it. She turned a few more pages, marveling at the delicate lines and brilliant color choices, at the fabric swatches Dorothy had pinned to the pages. It might be too painful for him to hang on to the sketchbook right now, but she was sure that someday, he would be sorry he'd thrown it away.

She'd slipped the book into her purse and had resumed her mission of tidying up the living room when Zane returned with a bottle of bourbon and two crystal highball glasses that looked out of place in his rugged bachelor digs. He balanced a ceramic cereal bowl full of ice atop the glasses. The make-shift ice bucket looked much more Zane-indigenous than the crystal barware.

"Those are fancy," she said, indicating the glasses.

"They were my mom's."

Even more than being her fairy godmother, Dorothy had been like a second mom to Lucy after her own mother passed when Lucy was just fourteen. Being here for Zane—looking in on him and making sure he ate something more than take-out pizza—was the least she could do to honor Dorothy's memory. Zane was big and strong and stoic. He wouldn't let on that he was hurting over his mom's passing, even though undoubtedly he was. That was why Lucy hadn't listened to him when he'd said he wasn't in the mood for company. That was why she'd shown up uninvited and pushed her way into his house.

"This wasn't hers." The ice clinked in the cereal bowl as he set it down on the table.

"Clearly. That ice bucket has *Zane Phillips* written all over it."

"Do you like bourbon? It's all I have right now. Bourbon or water. Or bourbon and water."

"Whatever you have is fine," she said. Zane picked up the bottle and poured them each about two fingers' worth of the amber liquid and she accepted the glass.

"I didn't know you were a bourbon drinker."

She wasn't. She didn't drink much and the strong taste of the liquor wasn't her favorite, but tonight it would do.

"There's a lot you don't know about me."

This time his right brow arched. A challenge. He didn't quite smile, but his eyes lingered on hers long enough to be suggestive. He made a *harrumphing* noise that seemed as if he was considering possibilities, or, at the very least, sizing her up. The thought of him thinking of her *like that* was thrilling and frightening, and she loved it.

Flirting with Zane was like a wild roller-coaster ride that twisted her every which way. Sometimes it made her feel as if she was about to tumble out of herself, or shoot straight off the edge of the universe. But when the car that was his attention finally delivered her to the station with a buzzing rush, she was always well aware she'd never been in any real danger of falling. Scratch that—she'd *fallen* a long time ago, but with Zane she knew she was never at risk of getting hurt. Because he didn't think of her *like that*.

"Want some ice?" he asked.

"Straight up is fine."

He touched his glass to hers. She followed his lead and tossed back the shot. It burned her throat as it went down. She fought the urge to cough. Finally, the fire settled into a gentle warmth that bloomed in her chest and then in her belly.

"Another?" Zane asked.

She nodded, even though she knew she needed to pace herself. She had no illusions of trying to hold her own with Zane, who had been drinking a bit too much since Dorothy died.

After he refilled her glass, she spooned three ice cubes into the bourbon. With ice, he wouldn't expect her to throw it back in one gulp again. Of course, she could've just told him she wanted to sip it straight up. For that matter, she could've just told him she'd had enough. He wasn't the kind of guy who would force her to do anything she didn't want to do. But she didn't want to make an issue out of it. Honestly, since Zane had been so closed-off lately, she wanted a little liquid courage—just enough to take the edge off and lubricate the hinges—so that she could open up and draw him out. Icing the bourbon would make it a sipping drink, a prop she could nurse for hours.

Obviously, Zane had no need for a prop. He tossed back another shot the same way he had the first one and went to pour one more.

"Whoa there, Bucky." She put her hand on his. "We don't have to polish off the entire bottle in the first five minutes. Why don't we eat something?"

"All I've done the past two weeks is eat," he said as he finished pouring himself a third drink. "People brought over so much food, I had to start freezing it."

"Ahh, which explains the pizza box," she said. "Makes sense. People bring food, you order pizza."

The right side of his mouth quirked. "Smart-ass."

Lucy shrugged.

The ladies of Celebration had seized the opportunity to cook for Zane. He was the most deliciously eligible bachelor in town. Every woman in town, young and old, loved Zane. Dorothy's passing, as sad as it was, was an excuse for them to bring him food and flirt. Lucy wondered if any of them had offered more personal means of comfort. Then she blinked away the thought. But not before pondering the possibility of him accepting said *comfort*.

No!

"I can only eat so much of Mrs. Radley's tuna-noodle surprise."

That's better. Let's talk about Mrs. Radley. She'd attended enough church potlucks and picnics to understand what he meant. Mrs. Radley's tuna-noodle surprise was infamous. The older the woman got, the more suspicious the congregation grew about the *surprise* mixed in with the tuna and noodles. Popular speculation wondered if she inadvertently used her cat's food in place of canned tuna. Only the bravest souls dared to try to figure it out.

"Did you actually eat it?"

"Of course. I appreciate her going to the trouble to make it for me."

Lucy winced. "And what was the verdict? Tuna for humans or fur babies?"

Zane thought about it for a moment as he added a few ice cubes to his drink, like Lucy had. "Hard to tell."

Lucy made a gagging sound and Zane laughed.

Maybe it was the bourbon that was lifting his mood, but she preferred to think it was her company.

"Chinese food sounds really good, Luce. Thanks for bringing it over."

The ice cubes clinked as he swirled his glass. He took a sip. As he watched her over the rim, she sensed something else in his demeanor shift. It made her senses tingle.

"I'm glad it sounds good. I know you've been showered with food gifts lately. I mean, I helped organize the deliveries."

Ugh. Stop talking. There's nothing wrong with a little silence.

She clamped her mouth shut so she wouldn't let it slip that she'd rescued Dorothy's sketchbook from the trash and ask him why he'd thrown it away. Or babble more inane thoughts about food gifts, like how when people died everyone wanted to feel useful. Help usually came in the form of neighbors dusting off recipes, firing up stoves and cooking way more food than anyone could reasonably consume.

Then after the funeral, life went on. People went back to the day-to-day grind and left the survivors hungry for more than a casserole, leaving them to make emotional decisions that resulted in tossing out beloved belongings that were too painful to look at now.

Tonight was all about showing Zane he wasn't alone. That he could lean on her. That she would keep him from making mistakes he'd regret later.

Really it sounded a lot more altruistic than it was because there was no place on earth she'd rather be right now than drinking bourbon, eating Chinese takeout and watching '80s movies with him.

And thank God she hadn't said *that* aloud, because it was definitely the bourbon talking.

Sort of.

Bourbon with a healthy chaser of truth.

"I'll get those plates." He set his drink on the coffee table and disappeared into the kitchen again. While he was gone, she moved several books about horse training and some industry-related magazines off the sofa, making room for them to sit.

Next, she pressed Play on the DVR remote. The opening scene of *Say Anything...* appeared on the screen. They didn't have to watch it now, but at least it would be background noise to fill any awkward silence so that she didn't feel the need to go on and on about everything that popped into her mind.

"If you don't want to keep these boxes here, I have room in the storage room in the barn," she said.

Earlier this year, Lucy had turned a dream into a reality when she'd converted the old abandoned barn on the property she'd inherited from her parents into a wedding venue called the Campbell Wedding Barn. During the first phase of renovations, she'd had the builder add on a good-sized, air-conditioned storage room.

"That way you can take it a box at a time and figure out what you want to do with everything."

He returned with the plates. "Thanks. But I'm good."

"Of course," Lucy said. "Zane, you're doing a great job. I know your mom is looking down on you from up there, appreciating all your hard work."

He frowned. "It is what it is. It has to be done. So I'm doing it."

"Be sure and let me know if you need any help sorting things out," Lucy said. "You know I'm here for you."

A small smile lifted the corners of Zane's mouth. He lifted his glass to her again. "Yes, you are. If I didn't say so before, I appreciate it."

"I know you do."

She thought about pointing out that sometimes she knew what he needed better than he knew himself, but she kept that bit to herself. Instead, she occupied herself taking the food out of the bag and opening the various containers. Better to show him than tell him. Her heartbeat kicked up a little bit. Yes, definitely better to show him.

Zane watched Lucy put her empty plate on the coffee table, kick off her flip-flops and pull her knees up to her chest. She looked small sitting there like that on his couch, with her long brown hair pulled back into a ponytail and her face virtually free of makeup. Since her attention was focused on the movie, Zane had free rein to watch her. It was a good thing, too, because tonight he couldn't keep his eyes off her. He loved her smile and her laugh and the way her eyes got big when the movie surprised her, even though she'd probably seen it dozens of times.

His reaction to her baffled him.

This was Lucy. *Lucy.* He had to be out of his damn mind to be looking at her like she was anything else than a little sister. Ethan Campbell's little sister. Ethan Campbell, his friend—a guy who was more like a brother to him than his own brother.

Lucy threw back her head and laughed at something in the movie that Zane hadn't heard. All that registered with him was the music of her laugh; it surrounded him, lifted him up, made him feel as if everything just might be okay. All he could see was the delicate curve of her neck and the way her upper lip was slightly fuller than her bottom lip. How had he never noticed that before?

Despite all his screwups, he must've done something right to have someone as good and pure as Lucy in his life.

"You doing all right?" She'd caught him watching her. He could see that her eyes were slightly misty from laughing.

"Fine," he said, even though he was feeling a weird kind of off-kilter right now.

He took a fortifying sip of his bourbon. The ice had melted and watered it down.

"Do you like the movie?" she asked.

"Not really." He smiled to make it clear that he was yanking her chain.

She shifted so that she was facing him, her tanned legs tucked underneath her. "We can switch to another one if you want."

He waved her off. "You're enjoying it enough for both of us. So no worries."

He took another sip and she mirrored him, picking up her glass and raising it to her lips. She closed her eyes as she drank. He had the ridiculous urge to reach out and run a thumb over her cheek to see if her skin was as smooth and soft as it looked. He didn't know because he'd never touched her like that.

This is Lucy, *man. Be cool.*

The world really was upside down if he was suddenly wanting to touch Lucy Campbell in ways that were decidedly unbrotherly, but he had to be honest with himself—that was exactly what he wanted to do. Even if he hadn't realized it until now. Since she'd been back in Celebration, it had never been so clear to him that Lucy was a grown woman who was decidedly *not* his sister.

He picked up the bottle and refilled his glass. As he started to set it down, he realized Lucy was holding out hers even though most of the original pour was still in it.

"Are you going to be okay to drive home later?" he asked as he filled her glass.

She shrugged. "We have a lot of movies to watch. And if I'm not, I can just spend the night here." She patted the sofa.

"Or I can call you a cab," he added quickly, as

much to chase away the thought of her spending the night. "People might talk if they see your car parked here overnight."

She laughed. "Let them talk. I didn't realize you were so worried about your reputation."

She held his gaze as she reached over to set her glass on the table and missed the surface by a fraction of an inch. Bourbon sloshed over the edge and the *ting* of crystal hitting the wooden edge of the coffee table sounded just before the glass fell. She caught it a split second before it hit the carpet. Good reflexes. She must not be that drunk.

In an instant she was sitting up straight, both feet on the ground, simultaneously blotting the spilled liquor with the white paper napkins that came with the takeout and examining the glass for signs of damage.

"Oh, my God. Zane, I'm so sorry. I can't believe I did that. I'm such a klutz."

"Don't worry about it." His hand touched hers as he commandeered the napkins—not so much because he was worried that there might be a stain, but because he didn't want her to feel bad. "It won't hurt the carpet. The bourbon will probably be an improvement."

He laughed.

"No." She shook her head, tears glistening in her eyes. "This is your mom's good crystal. I would've never forgiven myself if I'd broken it."

He stopped blotting. "It's just a glass. It's nothing special."

"Of course it's special. It's beautiful. And it was hers."

He shook his head. "I gave her the set for Christmas a few years ago, but she never even used them. I just took them out of their original box when I was in the kitchen."

Lucy blinked. "But they're so pretty. I can't believe she didn't love them."

"She did. Or at least she said she did. But she never used them because she said she was afraid something would happen to them."

"Yeah, someone like me would break them."

Zane waved her off. "Said she was saving them for a special occasion. Or, I don't know, something ridiculous like that. She was never particularly comfortable with nice things. God knew her louse of an ex-husband didn't even help with child support, much less spoil her with personal gifts."

Yeah, that was the poor excuse of a man Zane and his brother, Ian, were loath to call father. He preferred to not even think about the jackass who maintained that Dorothy had gotten pregnant with Zane on purpose. That she'd trapped him. He was so busy carrying around the chip on his shoulder, he seemed to think he was exempt from supporting his family. Never mind he'd gotten her pregnant again after they'd been married for a couple of years. It was always her fault.

After he'd divorced Dorothy, he'd married again and had kids. Zane didn't know his half brothers.

There were three of them and they weren't too much younger than him and Ian. He could do the math. He knew what that meant—that while his father was *away*, he was probably with his other family.

The real kicker was that Nathaniel Phillips had had the audacity to show up at Dorothy's funeral. After the service, Zane had confronted him, asking him what kind of business he thought he had showing his face. Ian and Ethan Campbell had flanked him like two wingmen. Ethan had herded Zane away, while Ian had asked Nathaniel to leave. And he did. He'd slithered away just as silently as he'd appeared.

Zane sipped his bourbon, needing to wash away the bitter taste in his mouth.

"My mom scrimped and saved and worked her ass off. Thanks to her, we never went hungry. We were always clean and clothed and we always had a roof over our heads. Our clothes were always from the thrift shop and the meals she cooked were nourishing, but never anything fancy. Although, if the Redbird Diner had pie left over at the end of her shift, she'd bring it home to us. I didn't even realize how poor we were until I was a lot older."

When Dorothy discovered she was pregnant and she and Nathaniel had gotten married, they'd moved in with her parents at the family's ranch on Old Wickham Road. A couple of years later, she'd inherited the land after her folks passed. When Nathaniel divorced her, they'd sold the ranch. Nathaniel got half.

His mom had lost her family home—his and Ian's legacy—and after paying attorneys' fees and relocating her sons, she had to struggle to make ends meet.

Nathaniel never paid a lick of child support. Dorothy had always claimed it would cost more to take him back to court than she'd get. But Zane suspected the real reason was that she didn't want to deal with the hurt of having to acknowledge that her husband had chosen his new family over them.

Out of sight, out of mind. Or at least she could pretend it was that way.

Zane's earliest and happiest memories were of working the Old Wickham Road Ranch alongside his granddad. Someday, he'd love to buy back the ranch. It wasn't for sale right now, and even if it was, he didn't have the money, since he'd used almost every penny he had to help his mom pay for her medical expenses.

Someday... But he knew that someday might never come. Dorothy's death was proof of that.

"She was a good woman, Zane. She was like a second mother to me after my mom died. Did you know she taught me how to sew? She was so good at it. Remember how excited she was when the traveling production of *Guys and Dolls* bought that dress she'd designed?"

Zane nodded.

"They offered her that wardrobe position with the show," he said. "She should've taken it and gotten out of here. Ian and I were out of the house. She could've traveled all over the country. I don't understand why she didn't do it."

Zane shrugged. "I wanted her to do it. I think everyone in this town wanted her to. But she said she was too old to become a nomad and *gallivant*."

He slanted Lucy a glance. "*Gallivant*. Her word."

He and Lucy laughed, but then they fell silent.

His mom had been a good, strong woman. Salt of the earth. You could rely on her like you could count on the sun to rise in the morning. But for all of her strengths, she didn't take chances. She'd worked her way up from waitress to manager of the Redbird Diner in downtown Celebration and she did clothing alterations and freelance sewing jobs in her spare time for anyone who was willing to hire her. That didn't leave a lot of extra time for fun.

When Zane turned fourteen, he'd gotten a job at Henderson Farms and helped his mom with expenses. He'd hoped that the extra income might make things easier. But somewhere along the way the person Dorothy Phillips could've become faded away, her potential lost to the demands of life, her fondest hopes and wants and wishes set aside in a box for a *special occasion* that never happened.

Lucy was quiet and Zane knew he should stop talking, but it was like he'd broken the lock on the compartment where he'd stuffed all his emotions, and everything was pouring out.

"You think you have all the time in the world to do all the things you want to do, but you don't." He took another swig of bourbon. "I have to get out of this town, Luce. I don't know what I've been waiting for. I'm thirty years old and I still don't know who I am or what I want. I mean, I know what I want, but I'm not going to find it here, not in Celebration."

Ironically, most people thought he was doing well. In fact, one woman who dated him was surprised to discover he wasn't rich. He'd owned a small horse ranch but had ended up selling the property after his mom got sick. The crappy insurance policy she had didn't cover all of her medical bills and there was no way in hell Zane was going to stand down and let her worry when he was sitting on assets he could sell and use to help her out.

Again, it wasn't that he was so magnanimous. Bridgemont Farms, the property that abutted his, had been pushing him to sell his land. Zane had been restless and they'd made it worth his while. They offered him enough money to allow him to help his mom and put a little bit in the bank; and he got to stay in his house because Bridgemont had hired him on as their general manager. Housing was a perk of the job. It was a means to an end, but there was no chance for advancement and Bridgemont's owners weren't interested in breeding champions.

Even though it was his choice to sell, it chafed to be limited by someone else's vision when he'd once had such big plans. Once, he'd dreamed of using the proceeds of the sale of his farm to buy back the Old Wickham Road Ranch.

Fate had different plans.

Even so, he still had an ace up his sleeve.

"Leaving isn't always the answer." Lucy pulled him from his thoughts. "Remember how I couldn't wait to get out of here?" Her eyes sparkled with optimism, or maybe it was concern. Zane couldn't tell. "I went away to school, and then I went to California, but nothing fit. Isn't it funny how once I came home, I found exactly what I'd been looking for and who I wanted to be."

"But you have roots here," he said. "You have your brother and your business. Of course you belong here. I have nothing keeping me here."

"I'm just saying you don't always have to go away to find your heart's desire. Sometimes it's right in your backyard, Toto."

She laughed at her own joke. He knew she was trying to cajole him out of his funk, but he couldn't even muster a chuckle.

He was happy for Lucy, that everything was working out for her. Of all people, he'd never begrudge her success and belonging. But she was six years younger than him. He needed to get his act together.

"I just have to get out of here—"

Zane's voice cracked and he swallowed the wave of emotion that was trying to escape on the coattails of his words. He hadn't gotten emotional since his mom had died. Until now, he hadn't realized that for the past two weeks he'd been pushing through life—through everything that had to be done—on some kind of foggy autopilot. Tonight it felt like the autopilot had died and he'd fallen from his fog into this hard new reality.

And he would've been okay, but Lucy was looking at him with those huge brown eyes. The gold flecks in her eyes that sparkled a moment ago had darkened a few shades. Her expression suggested she didn't know what to do with him. Hell, he didn't know what to do with himself. How was she supposed to know what to do with him?

That was why he was better off being alone until he'd sorted out all this emotional crap.

But Lucy's full lips quivered as if she was trying to figure out what to say to him. For a split second, all he wanted to do was lean in and kiss her so they didn't have to talk anymore. He wanted to lose himself in the taste of her, bury his face in her silky brown hair and keep going until he forgot about everything else that was going on in his life.

He cursed under his breath and balled up the soggy napkins he'd been using to blot the spilled drink a few moments ago. He tossed it aside before pushing to his feet and walking over to the window, where he could give himself some space to get his head on straight and stuff this damn sentimentality back into the box where it belonged.

"Are you okay?" she asked from behind him. His awareness of her had his body responding.

He didn't turn around. "Yeah, I—"

He needed to forget he'd ever wanted to do the

things he was thinking about to Lucy. What the hell was wrong with him? "I need some space, Lucy. I think it might be best if you left."

Because putting physical space between them—moving away from her—wasn't helping him shake it off. No matter how far away he moved, he couldn't unsee those lips or the way she was looking at him with those eyes... Worst of all, he couldn't unfeel the way his body was reacting to her.

As he stood at the window, he listened to the DVD playing in the background, but it was just noise because he hadn't been paying attention to it before now. He tried to think of anything else besides Lucy: his job, the part he needed to buy for his truck, baseball.

Strike one had been the thought of his mom never getting to celebrate that elusive *special occasion* that would've allowed her to use those *f-ing* fancy glasses. Strike two was the realization that the first ping of the damn crystal was marking her passing. Strike three was even though the first two strikes hadn't made him lose it, the way Lucy was looking at him was going to finish the job. Or make him do something he knew they'd both regret later.

He was a mess.

And it wasn't her fault. That was why she needed to just leave him alone.

"Zane?"

A violent clap of thunder had the sullen clouds bursting open and spilling rain in angry splats.

"Lucy, you shouldn't be here."

"Why?"

Why? He couldn't answer her, because if he did, he knew she would see right through him.

Thunder sounded again, this time it was like a fist pounding something hard.

"Surely you're not going to send me out in this weather," she said. "Not after all that bourbon."

He turned to face her. She was standing so close to him now, much too close, and he could feel the heat of her—of them—radiating in waves. "You're right. I'll go."

"No." She put a flat hand on his shoulder as if to stop him, and their gazes locked. "It's okay, Zane."

He wanted to ask her how she could think this was *okay*. Nothing about this was *okay*. He turned back to the window. The rain was falling harder now, punishing everything it touched.

"I'm sorry Dorothy didn't get to use the glasses," she said.

Her words hung in the air between them. He didn't have words of his own.

"Life is too short to wait for special occasions, or until the time is right—" She paused as a shard of lightning ripped through the sky. It was punctuated by another explosive clap of thunder.

"Life is too short to put off doing the things you want to do," she continued. "Don't you think so, Zane?"

Yes.

No!

Ah, hell.

She gently caressed his shoulders. He knew he should stop her, but instead he sank into it, his body needing her touch. She slid her hands down his arms, past the sleeves of his T-shirt. Goose flesh prickled in the wake of her touch, at the feel of skin on skin— her hands on his bare skin.

As she slid her hands around his waist and pressed her body to his, he closed his eyes and leaned his head back, letting her warmth soothe him, allowing it to melt his better judgment.

He wasn't drunk, though he might have been lightly lubricated. He knew what he was doing by letting her touch him like this. But did she?

"Lucy—"

"Shhhh." She leaned in and the heat of her sweet breath on his neck made him forget what he was going to say.

"Zane, we can't wait for someday. All those things we've always wanted to do…" Those lips were kissing his neck now and every inch of his body was responding. "We need to do them. Right now."

Somehow, she'd smoothly maneuvered so that she was standing in front of him, her back to the window, her arms around his waist. Maybe it was wishful thinking, but her eyes looked as clear and alert as they had when she'd first arrived. She'd had only one shot of bourbon and had spilled most of the second one he'd poured for her.

"Zane, I won't break if you touch me."

When he hesitated, she whispered, "I want you to touch me."

He put his arms around her and she slid her hands down to his butt, pulling him in so that his body aligned with hers. There was no way she wasn't feeling how much he wanted her.

His lips were a fraction of an inch from hers. He rested his forehead on hers.

"Lucy, I don't want you to regret this. I don't want you to think I got you drunk and took advantage of you."

"You didn't. I know exactly what I'm doing, exactly what we're about to do. I've wanted this for so long. I think you want me, too, Zane. Don't you?"

If you only knew.

His mouth found hers and he showed her exactly how much he wanted her.

Chapter Two

Six weeks later

Peeing on a stick was not supposed to be this complicated, but Lucy had found nothing easy about the task—especially when it kept giving her the result she did not want to see.

Her hand shook as she tossed aside the seventh stick that showed a positive result.

No! No! No! This was not happening. This couldn't be right. She could *not* be pregnant. But a little voice inside her told her that the odds of seven wrong results were slim to none. Her hands shook even more as she pressed the pump on the top of the liquid soap and turned on the warm water to wash up.

She stared at herself in the mirror as she rubbed her hands together under the warm running water.

She was pregnant.

What was she going to do?

She and Zane had spent one night together. *One night.* Six weeks ago. While she was well aware that it took only *one time* to get pregnant, they had used a condom.

How could this happen?

What was she going to say to him?

Lucy turned off the tap and dried her hands on the fluffy pink towel hanging on the rack behind her. The color looked astonishingly bright in contrast to the bathroom's white tile walls. Then again, all of her senses seemed to be amplified right now. She'd finally bitten the bullet and taken a pregnancy test after living in denial, chalking up what she now knew was morning sickness to food poisoning and the flu—a very, very long bout of the flu. Never mind she was usually as regular as the Fourth of July falling on July 4 every year.

She was certain the only reason she was late was because she'd been under a lot of stress lately. The Campbell Wedding Barn had been booked solid since *Southern Living* had featured the venue as one of "The Most Beautiful Wedding Barns in the South." She couldn't have purchased better advertising. So she had to admit her work stress was good stress. Too bad she couldn't say the same about her relationship with Zane.

While the air between them since that night wasn't exactly bad—in fact, they were sickeningly polite to each other—they had agreed that it would never happen again. Zane had been racked with guilt. "It's not you, Luce, it's me," he'd said. "It was wonderful, but I care about you too much for it to happen again. I don't want sex to ruin our friendship."

Umm...okay.

Not quite the morning-after talk she'd been dreaming of writing in her diary all these years. It was confusing and hurtful. At first, Lucy wasn't sure if it was his polite way of giving her the brush-off, but then he'd told her he was seriously pursuing job opportunities outside of Celebration. Rumor had it that a once-in-a-lifetime opportunity at a ranch in Ocala, Florida, was about to become available soon—literally, people stayed in those positions for life. So they were rare. He'd already sent in his résumé. There and to several other ranches that weren't in Florida. Because of that, he'd decided it was in their best interests if they just remained friends.

After she had gotten past the first few stinging moments of him dropping the it's-not-you-it's-me bombshell, he had reverted to acting like his old self again. Lucy had too much pride to let him know that their one night together had been simultaneously the best and worst thing that had ever happened to her. Although, for one insane moment, she had seriously considered countering with a friends-with-benefits offer—because even though her sexual experience wasn't vast—*OMG*—she knew a good thing when she, *umm…experienced* it. And that night with Zane had been *that good*. Out-of-this-world good. Ruin-you-for-others *good*. Total justification for a friends-with-*bennies* relationship, because now that she'd had a taste of Zane, she was starving for more.

But then hard, cold reality set in. Lucy knew herself well enough to realize she'd never be content with something so casual when she was in love with him.

Yep. She loved him.

But he didn't love her.

It was hard to wrap her mind around his saying that he cared about her too much for it to happen again. He promised he had enjoyed it. He'd even gone so far as to say it was his *best ever* and that was why they needed to keep things platonic.

Umm… It sounded like an oxymoron if she'd ever heard one. *It was so good; I never want to sleep with you again.*

That did not make one bit of sense.

Of course, she'd been upset and that was when he'd told her that he was one-hundred-percent certain that he was leaving Celebration and he would never ask her to give up her business to follow him and there was something about long-distance relationships not making sense. So they needed to be friends.

Now it had gone from friends-with-benefits to friends-with-a-baby.

How in the world was she going to tell him she was pregnant?

She'd been in love with Zane Phillips for as long as she could remember. And, yes, she might have had a daydream or two about having his babies, but she never would've gotten pregnant on purpose.

She covered her face with her hands and hoped that he wouldn't think she'd tried to trap him. When her hands fell, she stared at her pale face in the mirror.

He was going to think it was history repeating itself. And not in a good way.

It was no secret that there was no love lost between Zane and his father. Everyone in the community knew that Nathaniel Phillips was a bad husband and an even worse father—that was, when he'd bothered to come home. Before he'd served Dorothy with divorce papers, he'd been gone more than he'd been at home, leaving Dorothy to basically single-parent their two boys. When Nathaniel Phillips got remarried, it came to light that he had children with another woman who lived in Dallas. The one he claimed was the love of his life. Once Zane had confided in her that his dad resented Dorothy and him because Nathaniel thought Dorothy got pregnant on purpose, to trap him. He never loved her, and that was why he divorced her and married the woman he did love.

As far as Lucy knew, he was still married to her.

Lucy swallowed the lump that was forming in her throat. She would give Zane credit for being more evolved than that. She knew without even a second's hesitation that he wouldn't blame her or accuse her of trying to manipulate him. Of course, she had to prepare herself for the fact that this news was going to blindside him. She also had to accept the very real fact that he loved her about as much as Nathaniel Phillips had loved Dorothy. Although she wouldn't insult him by comparing him to his father.

"Zane does not love me," she said to her reflection, thinking if she said it out loud her heart would hear it and wake up to reality.

She said it again and listened hard.

The words echoed off the bathroom tile as she said them again. Reinforcement. She needed to make sure the words sank in, that she fully understood the reality of the situation. He might care for her as a friend, and they might be darn good together in bed, but he did not love her.

But of course, he was an equal partner in this, too.

Even if she had started it, because she had been the one who had gotten the love train rolling, because she knew Zane well enough to be certain that if she hadn't spelled it out, if she hadn't made it clear that not only was it okay for him to cross that line but she'd wanted him to make love to her, he never would have touched her.

Once the train was out of the station, so to speak, they had both been equally willing participants. She put her hand on her flat belly.

This baby was nobody's fault. The pregnancy was

unplanned and not ideal, and Lucy was still reeling from the shock of it, but none of that changed the fact that next March, she was going to have Zane Phillips's baby.

In the meantime, she needed to figure out how to tell him.

Chapter Three

Even if Zane hadn't readily admitted it to himself, on some subconscious level he'd known from the moment he'd picked up the call from Lucy that she was upset. He'd known by the tone of her voice that something was off, but she said she was simply having *one of those days* and didn't want to talk about it over the phone. She'd insisted that she was fine, but she needed to talk to him today and asked him if she could come over. He should've told her about the interview and asked if it could wait until he got back, but he didn't. Instead, he'd told her to come over.

She'd promised she wouldn't stay long. He certainly wasn't bringing out any bourbon and he wouldn't let himself be seduced by kung pao beef.

He used the word *seduced* lightly, though. It wasn't as if he was blameless when it came to their night together. He'd been weak, and he'd given in to his basest urges. He was perfectly willing to take full responsibility for what had happened between them. And along with that, he was fully prepared to make sure it never happened again. The last thing he wanted to do was hurt Lucy, or toy with her emotions. Even though he hadn't been cognizant of that the night of the bourbon, he was well aware now and it wouldn't happen again.

He knew he couldn't change the past and beating himself up over things he couldn't change was pointless. However, he could help them move forward.

In the past, if Lucy had called saying she needed to talk, he'd always made time. Now was no different.

And when he heard her arrive, he thought he was being authentic to their friendship when he answered the door, got a good look at Lucy and said, "You look like hell."

He instantly regretted it when she glowered at him.

"Gee, thanks."

"I mean, you're always beautiful," he countered. "You just don't look like yourself. Are you okay?"

She made a sound that was somewhere between a squeak and a harrumph. When she didn't come back with one of her usual quick-witted responses, he knew something wasn't right. Then again, telling a woman, whether she was a friend or lover—

or both—that she looked like hell was a boneheaded thing to do. He never had been good with words. He should just shut up before he dug himself in deeper.

"Come in. It's hot out there." He stepped back and held open the door, letting her pass into the living room.

They hadn't been alone like this in weeks—since *that* night. It hadn't been a conscious decision not to be alone together, at least not something they'd discussed. It was as if they'd mutually decided to stay in safe territory.

They'd seen each other in the company of others and had gone on as if nothing had changed. And it hadn't…had it? Or had he been so damn determined to make things normal again that he hadn't let himself see it any other way?

As Lucy stepped inside and he closed the door behind her, memories of the last time they'd been alone flooded back and his body responded.

He was leaving within the half hour. His bags were packed and waiting by the door. He could exercise enough self-control to be alone with her. But judging from the look on her face, that wasn't going to be a problem. Though she'd said she was fine when she'd called and asked if she could come over and talk to him, it was clear as the summer sky now that something was very wrong.

"Are you going somewhere?" Her face had softened to a look of concern, but the characteristic sparkle was still absent from her brown eyes.

"I am." It was all he could manage to say before a look of dawning replaced her look of apprehension.

"Did you get the Ocala job?"

He shook his head.

"It's just an interview."

Over the past six weeks, he'd had several interviews at various ranches in the South—he'd even had a couple of offers that he'd turned down because they weren't exactly right. There was always something amiss—either the salary had been less than what he was making now or some aspect of the job wasn't right. Actually, he'd been holding out for the job at Hidden Rock in Ocala, Florida. It was the real deal. The one he'd been waiting for. A chance to work with champion horses; potential for great salary; opportunity to do the kind of work he'd been itching to do. While he'd mentioned the Ocala prospect to Lucy in passing—that the ranch was looking for a general manager—he hadn't told her that he'd finally gotten a call for an interview. The stakes seemed so high and he was enough of a realist to know he shouldn't get his hopes up. It was a coveted position. He hadn't wanted to say anything to anyone, especially not to Lucy, until he had something more substantial to report.

A first-round interview, especially since it had taken them nearly two months to respond to his résumé, was not substantial.

But in typical Lucy fashion, she seemed to zero in on what he wasn't saying as if she was reading his mind. The thought was simultaneously comforting and unnerving, since everywhere he looked in his small living room, he saw reminders of the night that they had made love.

The window across the room, where it had all started. The couch that was right in front of them, where they had made love the first time. The hallway to his right, where they had somehow managed to walk while staying tangled up in each other on their way to the bedroom, where they had spent the rest of the night.

Reflexively his gaze fell to Lucy's lips and his groin tightened as he remembered how sweet she had tasted and how it had felt to explore her body.

No. He wasn't going to fall down that rabbit hole again, despite the way he was dying to reach out and pull her into his arms. It wasn't because things between them hadn't been good. Hell, they'd been great. Off-the-effing-charts great. And he had spent the past six weeks cursing himself for being so weak that night. He hadn't been himself. He had been out of sorts and overwhelmed by the magnitude of everything that was happening around him that he'd taken comfort in her when she'd told him she wanted him.

It wasn't an excuse, but it was a reminder that Lucy Campbell was his kryptonite.

That was why he needed to have a will of steel when he was with her.

He did not want to hurt her and he knew damn good and well that was what would happen if he lost control again. She deserved better than he could offer. Besides, if he got the job in Ocala, he would be moving. He wasn't about to try a long-distance romance. She deserved someone who had his life together, someone who could take care of her the way she deserved to be cared for. As far as he was concerned, Lucy was a princess and he was about the furthest thing from a prince anyone could imagine.

The truth sobered him.

Plus, given the mood she was in, she would probably slap the crap out of him if he did try to touch her again, and he would deserve it.

Yeah, it was a good thing that the car that Hidden Rock had hired to take him to the airport would be here any minute. He glanced at his watch to remind himself of that.

"Why didn't you tell me about the interview?" Lucy demanded, sounding more like herself.

He shrugged. "It's just a first-round thing. I'll be back the day after tomorrow. You wouldn't even have missed me in that short time span. In fact, you wouldn't even have noticed I was gone."

She frowned again and said in a small voice, "I would've noticed."

Of course she would have. If anybody in this town would've noticed he was gone, it would've been Lucy. And that was the perfect example of just how deeply in denial he'd been since he'd done the morning-after, let's-be-friends walk back, when he'd tried to explain it wasn't that he didn't want her. His life was a hot mess right now and the uphill climb he was facing to get himself back on track required all of his focus. There were the job interviews, plus his itch to get out of Celebration and start over. All of that added up to the fact that she just deserved so much more than he could offer her right now.

Things were starting to happen for Lucy. She was having success with the wedding barn. The last thing she needed was dead weight to drag her away from what was important in her life.

"Depending on how things went," he said, "you were going to be the first person I told when I got back."

Her mouth tilted up into a Mona Lisa smile and she looked sad for a split second. But then she lifted her chin and gave her head a quick shake. Again, the Lucy he knew and adored came shining through.

"So, tell me what they said," she demanded.

"They haven't said anything yet. That's why I'm going. To get the scoop. We're going to talk about all the details when I'm there."

She rolled her eyes, clearly exasperated with his reluctance to share what he knew. "Well, surely they gave you some indication of what the job entails. Didn't they? I mean, if not, you could be walking into a situation where they are looking for someone to muck out the stables. It would be a shame to go all that way only to find out you're highly overqualified."

"I'll take my chances," he said. "Especially since

I'm certain mucking out stables isn't part of the general manager's job description."

"What? Are you too good to muck out stables?" She smiled.

"Of course not. I have vast experience with that. So, let's just say I've already paid my dues."

They were quiet for a moment, looking at each other, and for a few seconds it felt as if nothing had changed between them.

"So, this is the one, isn't it?" she asked. "The job you really want."

It was. At least he thought so, but he hated to say too much, because it was a long shot. Anyone who was anyone in the equestrian industry wanted this job.

But who was he kidding? Lucy knew him well enough that if he said no, she would see right through him to the truth.

"Yeah," he said. "I'd love this job."

She drew in a deep breath and nodded. "Well, good. Since you'd been turning down offers left and right, I was beginning to worry that you were being too picky." She shrugged. "Or that you had finally decided you didn't want to leave me after all. Hey, how are you getting to the airport?"

"They've hired a car to transport me to and from Dallas," he said. "But thanks for offering."

"Who said I was offering?" Her smile was a little bit too bright and the dullness that had stolen the shine from her eyes didn't match it.

He wanted to ask if they were okay. Instead, he said, "If they weren't transporting me, I would've asked you to take me."

"Yeah, well, good thing, then," she quipped, her smile still in place. "I would've probably been busy."

The sound of the air-conditioning kicking on filled the vortex of weirdness swirling between them. Okay, so he'd screwed up by sleeping with her. This was too complicated. He could tell she didn't believe him when he said he cared too much about her for it to happen again. But he didn't want to hurt her, and if things were this weird after only one time, it was bound to only get more difficult if they did it again.

"What brings you all the way over here?" he asked. "Surely you didn't come here just to see me off."

"Sorry, Charlie. Given the fact that I didn't know you were going anywhere, that's not why I came over. But since you are leaving, it can wait."

"That sounds ominous," he said. "The car's not here yet, so what's on your mind?"

She bit her bottom lip and looked at him as if she was forming her words, then she shook her head. "No, it can wait until you get back. We don't have enough time to get into it."

"Get into it? Are you mad at me? Is this about what happened? Because, Lucy, I really do care about you. I'm so mad at myself. I don't want you to feel like I took advantage of you—"

"No, Zane. Stop. It's not about that—"

"You are perfectly within your rights to be mad at me. And that's okay. You can punch me if you want to. You can be mad at me for as long as you need to. But I hope it won't be too long because what's not okay is for us not to be okay—"

The sound of a honking horn cut him off.

"Your car is here. You need to go."

Dammit.

"I don't want to leave you like this. Will you please just talk to me for a moment? Tell me what's on your mind."

She had that look on her face again. The look that made him uncertain whether she was upset or maybe she really wasn't feeling well. Only this time, she put her hand up to her mouth as she closed her eyes and drew in a deep breath. She really did look like she was going to be sick.

"Lucy? Are you okay?"

"I—I'm sorry. I'll be right back."

She dashed off down the hall. He saw her close the bathroom door behind her, heard her turn on the water.

For a moment he wasn't sure what to do. He wondered if he should ask her if she needed anything. But suddenly he had a sickening realization of what she'd wanted to talk to him about. He understood perfectly.

He stood there for a moment, seeing stars and cursing under his breath as reality sank in.

Someone knocked on his front door. Zane answered, knowing it would be the driver. He steeled himself before speaking. It wasn't the driver's fault that this day had become a huge cluster of bad timing.

"Hey, man, sorry to keep you waiting," Zane said, to the guy. "I'll be out in a minute. Just as soon as I take care of something."

"Not a problem," the driver said. "I just wanted to make sure you knew I was here. The name's Raymond. May I carry your bags out to the car?"

Zane cast a quick glance over his shoulder to see if Lucy had emerged from the bathroom yet. Then his gaze fell to the time, which was displayed in glowing green numbers on the front of his DVR. It was already after four o'clock. His plane was supposed to take off at just before seven o'clock and he still had a half-hour ride to the airport.

"Thanks, but no. I'll bring them when I come out."

A moment after Raymond left, Lucy emerged from the bathroom, clutching a wad of toilet paper. Tears trailed down her cheeks and she shudder-sobbed when she looked at Zane.

He finally gathered his senses enough to go to her and put an arm around her and walk her to the sofa.

"Lucy, did you come over here to tell me you're pregnant?"

"The bride wants to drape every single wall in the barn in gossamer tulle," said Juliette Lowell. "From floor to ceiling. The ceilings are so high. I don't know if that's even possible. Is it?"

Juliette was Lucy's friend and neighbor. Her family had owned the property to the south of the Campbell ranch for generations. Now she was the owner of a wedding-planning business called Weddings by Juliette and was sending a lot of brides and grooms to the Campbell Wedding Barn.

Lucy shrugged. "We haven't tried anything like that before, but I suppose anything is possible."

By the grace of God, she managed not to snort. Because, yeah, after the turn of events in her life, anything could happen. Proof of that was that she was pregnant with Zane Phillips's baby. So, yeah, *anything* was possible. Well, maybe not *anything*. Not the good things—not that this baby wasn't good. She just hadn't had a chance to wrap her mind around it yet. And she had to do that and find out if Zane had gotten the job in Ocala before she could find the good in anything these days.

After Zane guessed her news, he hadn't exactly fallen to one knee and professed his undying love. Not that she'd expected that. Well, okay, she wouldn't lie. It would've been nice if he'd declared that his eyes had been suddenly opened and he realized he couldn't live without her. But he hadn't. Zane had reacted like a man in shock, and then he had gone to Ocala to interview for his dream job.

In all fairness, he'd offered to skip the trip. She'd insisted he go. Basically, she'd pushed him into the hired car that had been waiting to take him to the airport. And how about that—a *hired car*. As if paying for overnight parking wasn't more than adequate, Hidden Rock Equestrian had actually sent a car and driver. This ranch was no rinky-dink outfit. No wonder Zane wanted the job so badly.

A wave of nausea crested. She inhaled and rode out the feeling. She wasn't sure if it was caused by the pregnancy or the reality that Zane might really be leaving. But she couldn't think about that now because Juliette was saying something to her.

"What?" Lucy asked, feeling dazed.

Juliette was staring up at the apex of the pitched ceiling.

"I asked you what the ceiling measures at its highest point."

Lucy followed Juliette's upward gaze. "Oh. Umm... I have no idea. I mean, I could take a guess, but I don't know exactly."

It was a long way up, that was for sure. Tall enough to accommodate a second story, which was planned in another phase of the renovations Lucy would do to the place once she had generated enough capital. She'd already implemented phase one, which turned the formerly ramshackle barn into a place suitable for fairy-tale weddings. It had cost a lot of money to make a place hospitable while keeping the rustic integrity that was so popular with brides these days. She was taking the renovations slowly, keeping an eye on her margin so that she didn't get in over her head. With the way things were going, the steady stream of bookings would allow her to pay cash for the next phase of renovations sooner rather than later.

But now that she was pregnant, she might have to rethink things. She might have to use some of the money she was allocating for renovations for hiring extra help.

She was pregnant.

The reality kept washing over her in waves. Each time it hit, the force of it threatened to knock her down.

Juliette was frowning at her. "Are you okay?"

Again, Lucy wanted to snort. Because she was so far from okay right now she didn't even know where she stood. But the only thing she could do was say she was fine, because she and Zane hadn't had a chance to discuss matters fully. There was no way she could confide in anyone else about it right now. Not that she didn't trust Juliette. In fact, Juliette was one of the most trustworthy people she'd ever met.

But talking to anyone about it before she and Zane came up with a plan just wouldn't be right.

"I'm fine."

"You just don't seem as if you're all here today."

Oh, she was all here—plus some. Literally.

Since none of life's usual rules seemed to apply anymore, they might as well try something they'd never attempted before and cover the barn's walls in shimmery gossamer. At least it would be pretty.

"Is your client supplying the tulle or are we?" Lucy asked.

"I'll have to confirm with her," said Juliette. "But judging from how hands-off this bride has been, I'd wager that she'll want us to provide it. That's been her MO so far. She wants a miracle and expects us to make it happen. You know, no biggie."

Juliette laughed and Lucy forced herself to laugh right along with her.

Lucy could've used a couple of miracles herself.

Zane had nearly missed his plane to Florida because after he had guessed what was going on—that she was pregnant—he had insisted he couldn't leave her. That was why she hadn't wanted to tell him after she saw his bags sitting by the door and learned that he had gotten the interview. The only way she had been able to convince him to go was by pointing out that nothing would change while he was gone, she would still be pregnant when he returned and they would talk about it then.

Reluctantly, he'd gotten in the car, and he'd texted her an hour later to let her know he was at the gate and his plane was boarding. At least he hadn't missed it. But Lucy would've been lying if she said she wasn't a little worried about this job interview. This was the big one. Nothing had fit until now, and at the rate he'd been refusing offers, she was beginning to hope that maybe he really didn't want to leave. But just looking at his face as he told her about the Hidden Rock job, she knew this one was different.

After he'd arrived in Ocala, he'd texted her pictures: the Hidden Rock grounds, with lush, rolling green hills surrounded by miles of white horse fencing; the quaint downtown with shops that looked like something out of a European village. The occasional palm tree in the background added a bit of whimsy. Ocala looked regal and horsey. It looked like everything he wanted.

She felt terrible because a selfish part of her didn't want him to go, didn't want him to move on to a new life in Ocala without her. But even as she let the thought take shape in her head, she regretted it. Another part of her only wanted him to be happy, wanted him to get everything he wanted.

It nearly broke her heart to think that she would never be the one to make him that happy.

"Earth to Lucy." The words shook Lucy out of her reverie. Juliette was staring at her as if she'd missed something.

"Sorry, what?" Lucy asked.

"How are we going to get gossamer tulle all the way up to the apex of the roof?"

As both women looked toward the barn's ceiling, it was uncomfortably quiet. Lucy could feel Juliette's irritation. She needed to give her full attention.

"I don't know how we can do it unless we bring in scaffolding," Juliette said. She felt her friend's eyes on her, studying her. "Are you okay? You just don't seem like yourself today."

"I'm fine. I just have a lot on my mind," Lucy said, crossing her arms.

Juliette's scrutiny made Lucy want to squirm and

after another too-long stretch of silence, Juliette said, "I know what's wrong with you. I mean, come on, honey, it's obvious."

Lucy froze. What was obvious? How was it obvious? She wasn't even three months pregnant. How could Juliette know?

"Luce, you can confide in me," Juliette said. "I'm one of your best friends."

That was true. In fact, many moons ago, Juliette was almost family. She had been nearly engaged to Lucy's brother Jude. But that was a lifetime ago. Jude and Juliette hadn't seen each other in ages. Still, Juliette was her friend and she was one of the most intuitive people she knew. But Lucy wasn't about to tip her hand without being darn sure they were talking about the same thing.

"What do you mean, *it's obvious*?" She made her best are-you-crazy? face.

"Look at you. You're exhausted. You're a wreck. I know you well enough to see the signs."

Okay, there was intuitive and then there was freaking mind reading. This was whacked.

Had she let something slip? She'd been careful to confine all of her pregnancy research to her home computer. Even then, she'd searched incognito. She'd written the obstetrician's name, number and the date of her appointment on a piece of paper and had tucked it inside her wallet. She'd written only the time on her calendar, without explanation, so as not to double-book. However, she knew she hadn't been herself. Maybe she'd let something perfectly obvious slip.

Lucy decided to test the water. "You can't tell anyone, Jules."

A look of compassion spread over Juliette's pretty face. "Of course not, but, Lucy, this is a huge commitment. You need to know there's no shame in asking for help. No one is going to judge you."

Lucy didn't know whether to run or stand there and let Juliette see her burst into tears. Her eyes were already beginning to sting. She wasn't sure if it was from relief that she would finally be able to talk to someone about it, or because she wasn't sure how she was going to tell Zane that Juliette had guessed their situation.

"I mean, if they do judge, let them. Who needs them?" Juliette said. "I don't see anyone else raising their hands to help you with Picnic in the Park. They want to make suggestions and leave all the work to you."

Wait. What? She's talking about Picnic in the Park?

It was the annual Fourth of July event in Celebration's Central Park. It was a big, labor-intensive deal.

"When you volunteered to chair, I was afraid it was going to be too much for you to handle on top of everything else. Not that you're not perfectly capable. I just know how all-consuming a new business can be, and even though getting involved can be good exposure for your business, chairing the event is another level altogether. Not to be smug, but when you raised your hand, I saw this coming."

Lucy saw stars. She had nearly spilled the beans to Juliette when Juliette had been talking about something totally different. She stood there unable to speak, unable to breathe, because of the close call.

But it didn't matter, because Juliette continued, "That's why, if you'll have me, I would love to be your cochair. I was going to talk to you about it later, but since you brought it up, there's no time like the present, right? So what do you think? Want some help? May I be your cochair?"

Cochair?

Cochair. Holy…

That was when Lucy realized she was shaking. Her head was spinning and before she could stop herself, she enfolded Juliette into a hug that was laced with equal parts gratitude and numb relief. Relief for obvious reasons; gratitude because she was right that she had bitten off a little more than she could chew. Throwing a pregnancy into the Picnic in the Park/fledgling-business mix was going to add a whole new level to the challenge. But the event would be over in a few weeks and she'd cross that bridge when she came to it. For now, she would focus on how fortunate she was to have such a selfless friend in Jules. Her brother Jude had been an idiot to let her get away. But that was between Jude and Juliette.

When she and Zane did decide to share the news

of the baby, Juliette would be one of the first people she told.

As Juliette pulled free from the embrace, Lucy realized she had been holding on a little tighter than she should have.

Juliette frowned. "Are you sure you're okay?"

Lucy needed to get herself together—and fast.

"Yes. I'm fine. I'm great. I'm so happy that you offered to help me. It will make things so much better and it'll be so much more fun to work together."

"Luce, one of the first and most important rules of being in business for yourself is to know when to ask for help. You don't have to go this alone. Okay?"

The lump returned to Lucy's throat. She nodded, afraid that if she opened her mouth she might give herself away. She was already acting way too emotional for Picnic in the Park turmoil.

"Good, then," Juliette said. "I am going to get quotes on how much this gossamer-tulle endeavor is going to set back our client. I'll call John Rogers and see what he'll charge us to rent scaffolding. By the way, what are the dimensions of the barn?"

"About forty-eight by sixty feet," Lucy said, happy to ground herself in business talk.

Juliette pulled a notepad from her purse and scribbled down the information. "I'll call Maude's Fabrics and see if she can give us a deal on the tulle. I'm thinking wholesale. I'll let you know what I find out."

Lucy walked with her toward the doors.

"Let me know what I can do to help lighten your load with Picnic in the Park," Juliette said.

"Since you're offering, do you want to be in charge of herding Judy Roberts or Mary Irvine?" The women were longtime committee members who loved to make suggestions but never wanted to do the work.

Juliette's nose wrinkled. "Yikes, that's like choosing between bamboo shoots under the nails or eating an entire casserole of Mrs. Radley's tuna-noodle surprise. Let me ruminate on it and I'll get back to you. Maybe if I take long enough, you'll forget you asked me."

"Don't count on it."

After Juliette left, Lucy stood in the middle of the barn watching dust motes dance in a ray of sun streaming in from the skylight overhead. She put her hand on her flat stomach. This baby was going to change everything, but she was already attached to the tiny being growing inside her. They were going to be okay. No matter what Zane had to say, no matter where Zane ended up working and living, she and her baby would be fine.

During the two days that Zane was in Ocala, Lucy learned that she was much better off if she stayed busy. It gave her less time to dwell and obsess over the photos Zane had been texting her. She'd nearly driven herself crazy trying to decipher whether Hidden Rock was a good fit for him by looking at the photos and the level of his enthusiasm in his brief messages. It was like trying to read tea leaves. Since her to-do list was a mile-and-a-half long, she actually did need to stay busy so that she didn't fall behind.

The following night, she was in her office, a small nook toward the back of the barn, which she'd had built as part of the first phase of renovation, when her cell phone rang, startling her out of her zone. She glanced at the crystal clock on her desk. It was nearly eleven o'clock. She'd lost track of time. But who in the world would be calling at this hour on a weeknight?

She muted Harry Connick Jr. singing "It Had to Be You," which was streaming from her computer—her favorite music was old standards, and '60s and '80s retro tunes; tonight she was in a Harry mood—and fished her phone out of her purse.

A photo of Zane mugging for the camera, the default picture for his phone number, showed on the screen.

"Hey," she said. "What's going on?"

"Hey, yourself. I'm home from Ocala. Where are you?"

She leaned back in her chair and savored the butterflies incited by the sound of his voice. He must've just gotten in. And he was calling her.

She hadn't expected to hear from him tonight… tomorrow, maybe.

"I am in my office working. I didn't realize it was so late."

There was a pause on the other end of the line. "I didn't even think about the time. I'm glad I didn't wake you up. I'm actually outside the barn, can I come in and talk to you?"

Lucy sat up in her chair and looked around as if she might be able to see him, which was silly because the lone window in her office was covered by shutters. No one could see in or out.

"You're outside the barn?" she asked, smoothing her hair into place and licking her dry lips, then biting them to create some color.

"Well, I'm sort of in between your house and the barn. I'm in my truck. I knocked on the front door of your house and then I tried the barn door, but it's locked. I know it's late, but I really need to see you."

He *needed* to see her? *Needed to?*

An entire troop of butterflies swarmed in her stomach in formation.

Common sense warned her not to get carried away. It was doubtful that Zane had come to profess his love. But the hopeful side of her, the romantic in her who had been in love with Zane since she was old enough to know what love was, wanted to believe he had finally realized the love he needed—the love of his life—had been in front of him all these years.

Her old daydream suddenly played out in her head: Zane taking her hands, getting down on one knee and saying, "It's you, Lucy. It's always been you."

"Okay" was all she could muster and the word sounded more like a squeak than an invitation.

Okay? Ugh. Way to woo him with your quick wit and charm. No wonder it's never been you, Lucy.

She squeezed her eyes shut. The phone was still pressed to her ear.

"Meet me at the door," she said. "I'll be there in a sec."

She ended the call and gave herself a good mental shake before she got up and started toward the front door. This was Zane. *Zane.* The same guy who had always been so easy to talk to…before she'd slept with him. Now he seemed out of reach. Even though everything had changed, at heart they were both still the same people. Weren't they? Because of that, there was no need to get all goofy and moony and shy around him now.

After all, he'd seen her naked. She'd seen him, too, and *gawd*, he was beautiful.

The memory generated a slow heat that started at her breastbone and worked its way upward. She wished she could blame it on her pregnancy hormones, but she was experiencing a one-hundred-percent Zane-induced moment.

When she opened the door, he was standing an arm's length away from the threshold, a safe distance, in the outer reaches of the carriage lights' amber glow. The scent of jasmine from the bushes that grew in reckless abundance on the ranch loomed heavy in the humid air. Off in the inky distance a nocturnal creature hooted mournfully. She under-stood the feeling.

"Come in," she said.

He stayed rooted to the spot, looking stiff, with his hands folded one on top of the other in front of him.

Lucy shooed away a mosquito that buzzed be-tween them. She was just opening her mouth to say "Come inside so the bugs don't get in," but Zane spoke first.

"I've decided we should get married."

Zane realized he could have *proposed* in a differ-ent way. Maybe he could've tried to make it more ro-mantic, but this wasn't about romance and it wasn't really a proposal, in the traditional sense of the word. It was a partnership.

Didn't most marriages end up as partnerships any-way? The good ones did—the marriages that lasted involved two people who may have thought they were in love at one time, but they managed to hang on after the fireworks died and enter into something more permanent and lasting.

He'd never had that with anyone he'd dated. That was why he'd never considered getting married, but now that there was a child on the way, everything was different.

While he was in Ocala, he'd had a lot of time to think. He realized that he and Lucy were just skip-ping the doomed romance and diving straight into real life.

Too bad she didn't see it that way. She stood there in the doorway blinking at him, as if he had just suggested they put soap bubbles in Celebration's Central Park fountain. Or go swimming in the water tower on the outskirts of town. Both of which they had done when they were teenagers.

As they stood there in silence staring at each other, it dawned on him that his asking her to get married really was just as outlandish as soap bubbles in the fountain and water-tower swimming. Only, their situation deemed it necessary.

While he was away, he'd come to the conclusion that if pregnancy had to happen, he was glad it happened with Lucy. He liked her. He enjoyed spending time with her. Didn't it say something that not even sex could screw up their friendship? This could work.

Really, settling down wasn't such a bad thing. While he was away, he kept having a crazy thought that his past dating life had been like a big game of musical chairs: when the music stopped, you grabbed a chair. But it was almost a given that sometime in the course of things the song would end and you'd be without a chair. The pregnancy had left him without a chair. Or maybe another way to look at it was that he had been the one to claim the last chair.

Lucy was his prize. He cared about her more than anyone he'd dated. That was probably because they'd never dated.

"Just hear me out, Lucy. Please, can we talk about this?"

She stepped back, clearing his path, but still looked as if she smelled something bad.

"I know this isn't what either one of us wants, but it's logical," Zane said.

He heard her shut the door behind them. It echoed in the cavernous belly of the empty barn, which was empty of chairs and props because it wasn't set up for an event. He walked straight through to her office.

When she joined him in the office, he repeated the question. "Don't you think that's the logical thing to do?"

"I'm not going to marry you, Zane."

"What? Why not?"

He lowered himself onto one of the chairs across from her desk. She walked behind the desk and sat down.

"How was Ocala?" she asked.

"It was great. Pretty darn near perfect. Exactly what I've been looking for. But don't change the subject. You didn't answer my question. Why won't you marry me?"

She winced. She actually *winced* at the thought of marrying him. *Ouch.*

He knew he was no prize, but he was trying to do the right thing. He wasn't going to flake out on his child like his own father had. His dad had ignored his sons—at least the ones he'd had with Dorothy—and he'd treated her like crap. He never took responsibility, always blamed someone else, and had so many excuses for his shortcomings that Zane couldn't even keep track. Then the bastard had had the nerve to show up at his ex-wife's funeral.

Zane was going to be different. Different started by marrying the mother of his child and sticking around for the kid.

"Did they offer you the job?" Lucy asked.

"Not yet."

Lucy raised an eyebrow at him.

"I mean, it seemed to go well and I'm hopeful that they'll make me an offer. We talked money, I spent time with the staff, they showed me the cottage that comes with the job as a benefit."

She was still looking at him in that way that was so un-Lucy-like. The Lucy he knew and cared about would've cracked a joke by now. This Lucy was way too serious. But then again, he had just suggested they get married. It was a sobering thought. Obviously, she found the idea pretty unpalatable.

"So you're going to take the job if they offer it to you?" Lucy asked.

"Well, yeah. Especially now with circumstances being as they are." He put a hand on his stomach. "The money is good. A baby is expensive."

She nodded. "I've heard. Do you want something to drink? I have water and there's some soda in the refrigerator left over from an event we had last week."

He really could use a beer right about now, but she wasn't drinking alcohol and it just didn't seem right to drink in front of her. "No, thanks, I'm good."

Lucy stood up. "Well, I need some water."

She grabbed a glass off her desk and left the office. Zane followed her into the barn's kitchen. It was a functional space, a working kitchen with ovens and an industrial-size stainless-steel refrigerator that could accommodate food for wedding receptions and other catered events. He'd lent a hand with the construction to help save Lucy money. He got a boost of pride every time he entered the room.

He planned on helping her with phase two of the renovations—the second-story loft area she planned to build in the near future. Well, if he got the job in Ocala, he would help as much as he could whenever he was in Celebration. But they would cross that bridge when they came to it.

The humming of the fluorescent lights and the splash of Lucy pouring water into a glass from a pitcher she'd taken from the refrigerator were the only sounds in the room.

"I didn't expect you to do cartwheels at the suggestion of getting married, but I had hoped you'd be a little more enthusiastic."

She glared at him and he felt like an idiot. Of course—

"You probably need time to digest this," he said. "I've had a couple of days to think about this—about what we should do. I'm sure you've been thinking about it, too. But don't you think we owe it to our child to be a traditional family? That's the conclusion I keep coming back to."

"I think we owe it to our child to be the best parents we can be," she said.

"Exactly." He smiled at her. Now they were getting somewhere. "How do you feel about having the ceremony right here?"

She set down the glass on the counter with a thud. "You're either not hearing me or you're completely misunderstanding me. So let me make myself perfectly clear. I am not marrying you, Zane."

He really didn't think this would be so hard. When she stormed out of the kitchen, her rejection made him feel…empty. This wasn't a game, obviously. It didn't have anything to do with the thrill of the chase, but he had ended things with more women than he could count after they'd started pressing him for commitment. Now that he was willing to take the ultimate leap, Lucy couldn't get away from him fast enough. If he didn't know better, he'd think she hated him.

Maybe that was the problem. Maybe she did. He had let her down in a big way. They had both been weak that night. He should've been strong for both of them and stopped things.

That night came pushing back with a sensual punch that had his primal instincts warring with what he knew was right—what he knew he needed to do… Or not do.

Damn it all to hell.

He took a deep breath. Then he opened the cabinet, took down a glass and poured himself some water from the pitcher. He guzzled it down, the coldness of it giving him brain freeze.

There.

That was better.

He set the glass on the counter and walked back to her office.

She was sitting at her desk with her head in her hands and he hated himself for being the cause of her pain. "I know this is a lot to spring on you all at once. Why don't you take a few days to think about it—"

"I don't need time to think about it, Zane. I appreciate the sentiment of what you're trying to do. But I'm not going to marry you. It's not personal, but—"

"Of course it's personal. Everything about this is personal."

"Okay, so it *is* personal. What I meant was it's not *you*. I am not rejecting you."

"You just won't marry me. I see. No, I don't see. That makes absolutely no sense at all."

She swiveled in her chair to face him. "Yeah, that sort of has the same tones of your telling me our night together was the best sex you'd ever had, but it could never happen again." She clamped her mouth shut for a moment. "But that's beside the point. When I get married, it's going to be for love—mutual love—and it's going to last forever. It's not going to be a forced situation—like one of those fake Hollywood back-lot sets, where it's all show on the side, but really there's no heart or substance to it."

"I understand that you don't love me, but I can live with that, Lucy."

She laughed. She actually laughed out loud and he had no idea what the hell was so funny.

"You don't understand anything at all, Zane. At least not when it comes to you and me."

Now she was just talking in riddles. And even though this conversation was one-hundred-and-eighty-degrees different than any of the other conversations he'd had about marriage with anyone else, it did have one thing in common—it always seemed to come down to women speaking a different language, which was something he was obviously supposed to understand, but he didn't.

Another way that it was different was that this was the point when he usually exited. When it got too complicated or too heated or too heavy, he simply called it quits. It didn't take a genius to see the similarities between him and his old man, but now there was a baby in the mix and he wasn't going to take the easy way out like Nathaniel had.

"Obviously, I don't understand," he said, taking care to keep his voice calm and steady. "I asked you to marry me—you said no. I asked you to think about it—you said no."

"That's right." She looked so small sitting in her chair. She wasn't wearing any makeup and her hair hung loose around her shoulders. He could see shades of the girl he'd grown up with, but he couldn't sense in her the friend that she'd become. Right now she seemed like a stranger. And it was killing him.

"What I don't understand," he said, "is how you can just close your mind to the possibility. Lucy, we are good together, we've known each other forever. We would make such good partners. Most people get married because they think they're in love, when actually they're just hot for each other. That never lasts, and when it fades, some couples realize they don't even like each other very much. You and I, we like each other. We don't have to mess this up by complicating it with love and all that other emotional stuff. So think about it, okay? Would you do that for me?"

The look on her face was heartbreaking and for a few moments he thought he'd actually gotten through to her.

"Is that what you think of love? Is that all it is to you—just some hot-and-heavy sex, and when the sex isn't good anymore, it's all over?"

This was one of those trick questions. He knew it.

"I stand by what I said, Lucy. I believe the best foundation for marriage is friendship."

"So do I, Zane. But I also believe in love. You have obviously never been in love, have you?"

Okay. This was probably a good time to wind things down. It was late. They were probably both tired. She was getting into territory that he didn't want to touch.

"So let's back up here for a minute," she said. "You want us to get married. Let's say we did. Let's say you get the Ocala job. Of course you should take it. That means you'll be in Florida. My business that I've worked so hard for is here. Someone's going to lose and I have a sneaking suspicion you will expect me to pack up and go with you. So that we can live out our pretend marriage and be a pretend traditional family. Is that how your version of the story goes, Zane?"

He shoved his hands into his pockets. "Lucy, we should probably call it a night. My offer still stands. But let's discuss it when we're fresh. I probably shouldn't have come over here tonight. I just wanted you to know that you don't have to worry. That I plan on taking responsibility—for you and for our baby."

She stood up suddenly and slammed both of her palms on her desk. Her eyes glistened with tears. "You just don't get it, do you, Zane? Can't you see? All this baby and I are to you is a responsibility. I can't marry you simply to appease your sense of guilt."

Now she was full-on crying. He wanted to go to her, but he was frozen, rooted to the place he was standing.

"This isn't the way things were supposed to turn out." She was sobbing. "You really can't see it? You really have no idea?"

"Lucy?"

"Well, since we're laying it all out on the table, you might as well know. For as far back as I can remember I have dreamed of marrying you. Yes, Zane,

I have dreamed of being your wife and having your babies. But not like this. I am in love with you. I always have been and unfortunately I probably always will be. I thought going away, leaving Celebration, expanding my horizons and all that crap would help me get over you. That maybe I'd meet someone who would make me forget about you, but I didn't. I didn't quit loving you because that's the way I'm wired. And it really sucks that you don't love me. I get that, you can't just turn it on like a light switch. But what you need to understand is *that's* why I won't marry you. Because no matter how good of friends we are, a one-sided marriage, a marriage where I'm in love with you, but you're only there out of obligation, will never work.

"*That's* why I won't marry you, Zane."

Chapter Four

The next morning, Lucy opened her eyes and the magnitude of what had happened last night came rushing back like a punch to the gut. She bolted upright in bed and pressed her hands to her face.

Oh, my God, what did I do?

She had told Zane that she'd been in love with him her entire life. That was what she'd done.

Sure, Zane had provoked it by asking her to marry him, but— *Gaaah!*

She squeezed her eyes shut, as if she could obliterate the nightmare. Because that was what it was— the stuff that nightmares were made of. Only, this was real. It hadn't happened in a bad dream. It had played out in living color between her and the only man she had ever loved.

She ran her fingers through her mussed hair, tugging a little too hard. She couldn't blame her slipped filter on the pregnancy hormones because she knew it wasn't the truth. She wasn't going to use this pregnancy as a crutch, an excuse for saying and doing things she shouldn't have done.

Instead, she tried to convince herself it was no big deal, that given the present circumstances, it was something he needed to know. Didn't he need to know she loved him? But it didn't make her feel any better. Because *no*, he didn't need to know that.

Major *TMI.*

It wouldn't change anything. Well, the only thing it might do was make life more difficult. It was as if something had possessed her and ripped the confession right out of her heart.

No, enough blaming everything else. She had betrayed herself by not having better self-control.

Oh, God. Oh, God. Oh. God. No.

Again, she covered her face with her hands, pressing her fingers into her eyes. How could she ever face Zane again?

She wasn't sure which was worse—having to face him, or worrying her confession might have sent him packing. She wouldn't be one bit surprised if last night's episode of *True Confessions: Lucy Spills the Goods* had inspired him to hightail it back to the airport and hop on the next flight to Ocala.

But she knew him better than that. Of course that wouldn't be the case. He wouldn't run. Besides, they hadn't offered him the job yet. Still, they would soon enough, and if he needed one more good excuse to add to all the reasons he wanted to leave Celebration, surely her blurting the *L* word would be all the reason he'd need.

She took a deep breath and let her hands fall from her face. She tried to blink away the blurriness caused from pressing so hard. Once she could see straight again, she realized the world was still turning; the sun had risen and was shining in through the spaces between the white plantation shutters, casting light and shadows, just like it did every sunny morning.

Obviously, life would go on despite her deep mortification. She resisted the urge to lie back in her bed and pull the pink-and-white duvet over her head. There was no time to wallow. She had a Picnic in the Park meeting and she was going to be late if she didn't get up and get a move on.

The situation was what it was, she thought as she padded on bare feet across the hardwood floors, into the en suite bathroom. She braced her hands on the counter and forced herself to take a good, hard look at herself. There was no taking back the words. No changing what had already happened. So she might as well get over it. She would need to figure out what kind of damage control she should implement so that they could move on accordingly. She wasn't going to marry a man who didn't love her and Zane would have to come to terms with that.

But for now, she had a meeting she needed to prepare for. She turned on the cold water and splashed her face. Even the bracing tap couldn't wash away the memory of Zane standing there, one cool cowboy. After her confession, he'd stood there stoically for a moment, and then, without missing a beat, he'd acted as if he hadn't heard her. He'd simply repeated his original suggestion that she take some time to think about getting married and they'd talk about it later. Then he left.

That was it. On the surface, it seemed like it hadn't even fazed him. After he'd gone, she'd stood there for a few minutes wondering if he'd even heard what she'd said. But of course he had. She'd blurted it loud and clear and now he knew.

It was simmering underneath and that was what made it worse. It would've been better if he had acted shocked or repulsed—okay, maybe not repulsed. That would've been worse. But some kind of a reaction would have been better than none at all.

Did he think by not acknowledging what she said it would simply go away?

Maybe that wouldn't be such a bad idea.

Maybe she should borrow a page from his playbook and pretend like it hadn't happened. Pretend like she hadn't made a total fool of herself, that she hadn't said anything at all.

If only.

She grabbed her toothbrush and squeezed out a pearl of toothpaste.

No, the only way to handle this would be to face it head-on and…and then what? Dissect the fact that she loved him and he didn't return her feelings? What more was there to say? She understood. She didn't need to make it any more painful than it already was.

Loving someone wasn't a heinous act.

I love you.

Boo. Hiss. You terrible person. How dare you love me?

In fact, if he had a problem with it, wouldn't *he* be the jerk?

But Zane wasn't a jerk. He'd never been a jerk to her. Not even when he'd told her they needed to just be friends. Even then, he'd been warm, and tender, and concerned about her. And he had been the one to first reach out in friendship, proving that nothing had changed between them.

Even though *everything* had changed.

She continued the mental pep talk as she brushed her teeth.

Plus, he was the one who had suggested that they get married. Of course, he had basically acknowledged that it would be a loveless marriage—and in his eyes, that was the beauty of the arrangement.

Then she had to spoil it all by saying "I love you." Ugh. Great. Now the song "Somethin' Stupid" would be stuck in her head for the rest of her life.

She rinsed her mouth and toothbrush and returned

the brush to the rack. As she showered and got ready for the day, she decided the best plan was to do nothing. She'd give Zane some space. Maybe her great revelation would make him think twice about the proposition he'd presented last night.

As she sat at her dressing table, she pulled up her music streaming app on her phone and found the Frank and Nancy Sinatra version of "Somethin' Stupid," the song that had earwormed its way into her brain since she'd inadvertently quoted it earlier. She wallowed in how perfectly the lyrics fit her situation as she put on her makeup. For balance, next she played "I Told Ya I Love Ya, Now Get Out." It fortified her.

The reality that had been swimming in her subconscious, just below the surface, came up for air: it wasn't supposed to be like this. In the past, when the going got tough, she'd always fallen back on her daydreams. In those fantasies, Zane had loved her. He would look at her and say, "It's you, Lucy. It's always been you." And then he would kiss her, they'd get married and they would live happily ever after.

But the reality of the situation was that Zane didn't love her. He was willing to marry her out of obligation.

She supposed she could take a chance that he might grow to love her—maybe she had enough love for both of them. But what would happen if the right woman came along and he did fall in love with someone else? He would be saddled with her and their child. Given all that Zane had gone through growing up, she didn't think he would cheat—he probably wouldn't leave her, either. But what kind of life would that be, stuck in a loveless marriage? Stuck with someone who you liked a whole lot but just couldn't love? It wasn't his fault. The heart wanted what the heart wanted. It wasn't as if he could reprogram himself to feel different.

But at the same time, she was only human and she couldn't help but fear being the one who was in love...the vulnerable one. The thought of such a lopsided relationship made her feel sad and sick. She'd experienced morning sickness enough to know the difference—this was what it felt like to be heartsick in a hopeless situation. For a hopeless romantic to have her fears of being unlovable validated.

The best thing she could do would be to do nothing. She would let Zane come to her, and when he did, she would tell him she'd had a chance to think about things, but she hadn't changed her mind.

Surely, he wouldn't argue with that, would he?

The Picnic in the Park event committee met in Central Park in downtown Celebration for a walk-through. Lucy was a visual person and she wanted to see the area where the community picnic would take place to get a better idea of where the games, tents and stands would go. They needed to make sure they had plenty of parking for those who were driving in, but they still needed to reserve an adequate amount of space for the fireworks and the food-truck brigade that was gaining a popular following in Celebration.

"How many tables do you think we need for the hot-dog eating contest?" Mary Irvine asked. "Last year Pat Whittington complained for a good six months that he didn't have enough elbow room and that's why he didn't win."

"Pat Whittington is a sore loser," said Sandra Riggs. "His not winning had nothing to do with whether or not he had enough elbow room. Maybe he should stop complaining, and stuff more food down his gullet. If nothing else, it would shut him up."

Sandra and Mary laughed. Lucy could see that this could digress fast, so she quickly steered them back on task.

"That's the reason I've asked people to sign up for all of the contests by the end of the day on July 1," said Lucy. "That way we'll have a better idea how much space we need for each event and we won't have to push people together."

Judy Roberts frowned. "You know we've never done it that way before…" She slanted a knowing look at Mary, who pursed her lips and raised her brows. "Word on the street is people think preregistering for the games sucks all the fun out of it."

Judy shrugged. "There. I said it. It needed to be said. I've been on this committee for as long as Picnic in the Park has been around and that's just not the way we do it."

Carol Vedder put her hands on her slim hips. "If

you've been on the committee that long, Judy, how come you've never wanted to step up and chair the event?"

Carol looked smug. "There. I said it. It needed to be said. You always have such good ideas, but you never want to do the work to get them done."

Judy blanched, and even though Lucy could have hugged Carol's neck for saying exactly what she was thinking, she did her best not to appear as if she was taking sides.

"It's okay. I appreciate everyone's help and all opinions are welcome," said Lucy. "Even so, I'm going to try out preregistering this year. If it doesn't work, the committee can always do away with it next year."

"I think it's a good idea to ask people to preregister," Carol chimed in. "It will make things so much easier for the volunteers on the day of the event."

Carol beamed at Lucy and suddenly Lucy wondered what the woman was up to. Carol could be just as challenging as the rest of the long-standing committee members. Why was she being so nice? What was she up to?

She knows you're pregnant.

The thought sprang into her mind unbidden. It was ridiculous. There was no way Carol would know. Just like Juliette, who knew her much better than Carol, hadn't known. Lucy had gone all the way to Dallas to purchase the pregnancy tests and she'd taken care to dispose of them in a public Dumpster when she'd been out of town on business. Besides, if Carol knew, she would undoubtedly be too busy broadcasting the news to anyone who would listen to be this nice.

Bottom line: there was no way Carol could know. Lucy forced herself to shake off the ridiculous thought and wrap up the meeting. Sure enough, as soon as they were finished and heading toward their cars, Carol caught up with her.

"Lucy, darling," she chirped. "Do you have a moment?"

Lucy's blood ran cold. There was no way she could know. She stopped and smiled. "Sure. What's on your mind?"

"Are you seeing anyone these days?"

Lucy took a steadying breath. "Why do you ask?" She took special care to infuse sunshine into her voice so that she didn't sound defensive.

Carol smiled like a Cheshire cat. "Because if you are unattached, I have somebody special I would like you to meet."

Oh.

Ooh.

What in the world was she supposed to say to that? She was in no position to meet anybody. She was in no position for anything that would make her life more complicated than it already was.

"I am sort of…seeing someone."

"What do you mean *sort of*? Either you are or you aren't."

"It's complicated," Lucy said.

Boy, was that ever the truth. It couldn't get much more complicated than this—she loved Zane, but Zane didn't love her. Zane wanted to marry her, but she didn't want to marry Zane. And the cherry on top—she was pregnant. Nobody in his right mind would want to date a woman who was pregnant with another man's baby.

"Oh, honey, why do so many nice girls like you allow themselves to be in situations that are *complicated*? Isn't that just another way of saying a guy is afraid of commitment? I'd say if he's so *complicated* that he can't recognize a good catch like you when you're standing right in front of him, he doesn't deserve you. I want you to meet my nephew, Luke. He will treat you right and he's a good-looking guy. A veterinarian. Lives in Houston. A good catch. Just like you."

Carol wiggled her brows and fished a photo out of her wallet.

He was, indeed, a good-looking guy. Even so, Luke might be the catch of the century, but he wouldn't think much of her when he found out she was pregnant.

Talk about *complicated*.

That was when something clicked into place—it really didn't break her heart to know that other men would find her unappealing, or even damaged, after they found out she was having a baby on her own.

She didn't care. She really didn't care. And it was the most freeing feeling she'd had in ages.

Her baby would be family and as far as Lucy was concerned the love of her family was all she needed.

Her phone dinged, signaling an incoming text from Zane. Her heart leaped at the sound of his special text tone, but she left the phone in her purse. She'd look at it when she got in the car.

"Carol, I'm sure Luke is a wonderful man. And I appreciate you thinking of me, but I have too much on my plate right now with work and the picnic committee. I'm sure you understand."

"Honey, just meet him. That's all I'm asking. I'm not saying you have to marry him."

This time Lucy's phone rang. It was the ringtone she had assigned to Zane. Thank God nobody knew her assigned rings. "I have to take this, Carol. I'll talk to you later."

Lucy turned toward her car before the woman could say anything else.

She waited until she was a few feet away before she answered Zane's call.

"Hello?" Her heart was beating like mad. She took care to keep her voice low.

"Hey, it's me. I need to see you tonight. May I come over?"

Just like that. As if nothing had happened last night. She should've said no. She should've told him to leave her alone. The words to the song "I Told Ya I Love Ya, Now Get Out" played in her head. Because he wouldn't be popping in like this once he moved to Ocala. And even though the words and her empowerment song were in her head, she said, "Sure. I'll be home after six."

"Why have we never dated?" Zane asked as he stood in Lucy's kitchen helping her chop the vegetables he'd brought her from the crate that Mrs. Winters had brought him from her garden.

Lucy's head jerked up and she looked at him as if he had just started reciting the words to a Dr. Seuss book.

"Because you never asked me out." She sounded a little irritated, or maybe she was just perplexed. He seemed to have that effect on her these days.

When he'd handed the vegetables to her in the rumpled brown paper sack, they'd seemed like a very inadequate peace offering after the run-in he'd had with her last night.

He would've given anything for her not to hate him. Anything.

Anything except his love, which was the only thing she really wanted and the one thing he wasn't able to give her, because he was incapable of falling in love. He had no doubts now, because if anybody was worth loving, it was Lucy.

Even so, he couldn't lie to her. She deserved better than that.

But she'd seemed pleased with the vegetables and

maybe even glad to see him—or at least willing to see him. And she had invited him to stay for dinner.

"Why have you never asked me out?" she countered. "Oh, wait, I know. Because you were too busy putting the moves on Bambi and Bunny and Bimbo—sometimes all at the same time—to fit me in."

"I never dated anybody named Bambi or Bunny or Bimbo."

"Yes, you did, because that's what I called them."

"Remind me to not let you choose the name for our baby."

"I will choose a lovely name for our child."

"*We* will choose the name," he said. "Luce, we're in this together."

The joking fell silent and the only sounds in the kitchen were the hum of the refrigerator and the sound of the knife hitting the cutting board. She had put him to work chopping the tomatoes, carrots and a cucumber for a salad that would go with the spaghetti and turkey meatballs she was making for dinner.

Now was as good a time as any to finish saying what he had come to say. But damn if he wasn't nervous. What the hell? When was the last time a woman had made him nervous? But he was. Dry mouth. Racing heart. Overthinking.

Get over yourself, man.

He set down the knife and turned to face her. "Obviously, I've gone through periods of my life where

I was looking for a *different* kind of woman. Different than you, I mean."

Her right brow shot up in a way that made him a little crazy.

"You keep digging yourself in deeper, don't you?" She was goading him. "At this rate, by the end of the night you'll probably be pretty close to six feet under. So, how am I different from your usual cast of fluffy woodland pets, Zane?"

But it was a good kind of crazy, one that, if he hadn't been so dense, might have made him realize a long time ago they had something good. That she was a good kid…er, *woman*. A good *woman*. Lucy may be a few years younger than him, but she was most decidedly a woman now. He had to keep an iron grip on his willpower so as not to let his gaze fall to her oh, so womanly curves, which were making him more than a little crazy, too.

He cleared his throat. "I don't care about the past, Lucy. The past doesn't matter. I care about now and what I came here to say is that I think we should try dating."

She scrunched up her face as if it was the most distasteful suggestion she'd heard in a long time. It wasn't the way he thought she'd react. Why should he be surprised when she always kept him guessing?

Not even twenty-four hours ago she'd told him she was in love with him. He knew better than to bring that up, but damn it all to hell, she was more confusing than any woman he'd ever met. She was like a riddle he couldn't figure out. A challenge that both thrilled and scared him to death.

The last thing in the world he ever wanted to do was hurt her. And he'd done that already. He'd let her down by letting *this* happen. He'd wanted her in the worst way the night they'd hooked up. He should've been stronger. He should've been strong enough for the both of them. Strong enough to walk away. If he had, then they wouldn't be where they were right now.

A strange feeling washed over him, because the more time he had to get used to where they were right now, the more it didn't seem like such a bad place.

"What did you say?" she asked.

"I said I think we should try dating."

"Other people? I think you've already established that." Her face fell and she turned back to the stove and stirred the spaghetti sauce.

"Lucy, I'm talking about us. I think you and I should try dating. Each other. You and me."

She didn't turn around. She just kept stirring the sauce. One of those sassy, old-fashioned songs from the '60s that she liked so much played in the background. Something about windmills and the mind. Whatever that meant.

Finally, when he couldn't take her silence any longer, he said, "Will you say something? Please?"

He saw her shoulders rise and fall, but she still didn't turn around. So he walked over to her, bridging the distance. He wasn't sure if he should touch her. He wanted to, but that was for purely selfish reasons. No, it wasn't. He wanted to comfort her, but he was afraid that, again, his good intentions would lead them straight into hell.

"Lucy, look at me."

She raised her hand to her face before she turned around to face him. He could virtually see her stiffening resolve.

"You want to date me? Why?"

Now she did look truly irritated.

"Because you and I need to get to know each other on a different level. I mean, we know each other well. In some ways, you know me better than any of the past fuzzy woodland creatures, as you called them."

"Fluffy woodland pets," she amended. Then she shrugged. "Although if you think *creature* is a better word, then go for it."

She rolled her eyes and chuckled a little, but it was dry and humorless. Still, he could sense that she was softening. He understood her hesitation. In fact, all day long it was all he could think about. She was all he could think about. Her and her earnest declaration of love.

Lucy *loved* him. How could he have missed that? How could he have been so completely blind to something that now seemed so completely obvious? After he'd left her, he'd sat with the newness of it most of the night. Even when sleep had found him, and it had come in fits and starts, he would wake up with the echo of her words in his head. And every time he closed his eyes he would see her heartbroken face, as if it had been imprinted in his mind.

More than anything, he wished he could return her feelings. But even though he cared about her—more than he'd ever cared about any woman he'd dated—he couldn't ever recall a time when he had been in love.

He was a lot of things, but he wasn't a liar. And telling Lucy he was in love with her would have been a lie. But that didn't mean he couldn't try. That didn't mean he couldn't treat her like the woman he wanted to marry. Like someone he could…love.

"You and I have sort of been all over the place. We grew up together. We're friends. We made love—"

She cringed, closed her eyes and made a face, but he wasn't sorry he'd said it.

"Lucy, we did. There's no sense in trying to sugar-coat it or pretend like it didn't happen. We did and it was great. And now we're having a baby. But I think we need to back up a little bit. We need to start over and build our relationship from the ground up. Even if you won't marry me, we need to know each other on a deeper level so that we can successfully coparent. That's why I think we need to try dating each other and getting to know each other as a man and a woman. So what do you say, Lucy Campbell—will you let me take you out on a date?"

Chapter Five

Lucy agreed to a date on one condition: things didn't get weird. Or any weirder than they already were. No flowers. No dressing up. No fancy dinners. That wasn't them, it wasn't who they were. Things like that upped the odds that things between them would be strained and…get weird. Things like that screamed *expectations*! The last thing she needed right now was to get her hopes up about anything. Especially when it came to Zane Phillips.

It was logical to put one and one together and expect two. It would be too easy to think that his willingness to downsize a marriage proposal to a first date, rather than getting mad and not speaking to her, might mean that Zane hadn't ruled out the possibility that he could love her. At least he was trying. He hadn't given up on her.

There she was, getting her hopes up. In this case, her better judgment warned that one plus one was more likely to add up to expectations. She always had hated math.

They were going downtown to get ice cream and take a walk. It would be simple and informal. Unpretentious. They could be themselves and just be.

Freshly showered, Lucy had blown out her hair and brushed some Moroccan argan oil through her brown locks to make them glisten. She'd kept her makeup to a minimum, just enough to make her look polished and put together—like she'd made an effort. Making an effort didn't mean she was making more out of this than she should. Nope. Absolutely no expectations here, she thought as she returned the lip-gloss wand to the container and gave herself a once-over in the mirror. In fact, she was doing this for herself because it made her feel good and everyone knew feeling good was the best armor a woman could wear.

As she stood in front of her closet, surveying its contents, her phone dinged, alerting her to a text. It wasn't Zane's text tone, but she took a look anyway. It was from Chelsea, her sister-in-law-to-be.

If you don't have plans this afternoon, do you want to go look at wedding shoes with me?

Chelsea and Ethan were getting married in a couple of weeks. The ceremony and reception were going to be at the Campbell Wedding Barn. Chelsea, who had relocated to Celebration, Texas, from London, was a real-life British noblewoman who had gone to college—or *university*, as Chelsea would say—with Juliette. Aside from her accent, people would never guess that Chelsea came from such a highbrow background. She was about as down-to-earth as anyone could imagine—except when it came to shoes. She had a penchant for good shoes—expensive shoes. Hence the reason the wedding was two weeks away and she had not yet found the shoes she would wear with her dress.

Lucy racked her brain for a moment, trying to figure out what to tell Chelsea about why she wasn't available. She couldn't say she was working, because with her luck she'd run into her downtown, or Chelsea would swing by the barn—and it wouldn't be the truth. Why did she feel she had to lie? Why not just tell her the truth?

Lucy texted back. Next time? I told Zane I'd hang out with him this afternoon. I doubt he would enjoy shoe shopping.

Chelsea responded quickly. No prob. Tell Zane I said hello.

See, Chelsea hadn't thought it was weird that she and Zane were getting together.

So, stop making it weird.

She was trying, but the fact remained that it shouldn't be this hard. She knew it was fanciful, but she wanted Zane to fall in love with her—like when the prince looked at Cinderella and realized she was his one true love. Too bad she didn't have a fairy godmother to help her out. If Dorothy was still here…what would Dorothy think of their situation?

There was no time for daydreams. He would be there soon and she needed to finish getting ready.

Before she chose a dress, she streamed "Somethin' Stupid," because making fun of herself was the best way to stop taking herself so seriously. She reframed her focus and selected a feminine yellow print sundress from her closet and a pair of cute cowboy boots to go with it.

The dress was fun and flirty and made her feel girlie. She debated whether or not to curl her hair, and even went as far as firing up her curling iron, but in the end she opted for pulling it back into a ponytail. Curls would look as if she was trying too hard. She probably was, but Zane didn't need to know that. He just needed to be captivated by the finished look.

It ended up being a good thing that she'd opted for the ponytail, because a knock sounded at her front door. She glanced at her watch.

Right on time.

She pulled the boots on and made herself slow down and take her time getting to the door, when what she really wanted to do was rush. Once she was there, she paused and took a deep breath before she turned the knob.

Zane stood on her front porch holding a…baby cradle?

"What are you doing? Come inside, quickly." Lucy tugged his arm and nearly made him drop the cradle, which was heavier than it looked, because it was one of those solid-wood, sturdy old-fashioned pieces of furniture. The type they didn't make anymore.

What the hell?

"Careful," he said as he cleared the door, but not before grazing the doorjamb with one of the runners.

"Someone might see you," Lucy said as she closed the door behind her.

"Am I not supposed to be here?" Zane asked. "I thought we had a date."

Lucy frowned at him. "Of course *you're* supposed to be here. Just not with a baby bed. That's not exactly a typical substitution for first-date flowers."

He set down the cradle on the living-room area rug so that it didn't scratch her hardwood floors.

"I thought we agreed that you didn't want me to bring you flowers."

"I didn't want you to bring me flowers. But that doesn't mean I wanted a baby cradle instead. Zane, it's too soon. How am I supposed to explain why I have baby furniture in my house? I haven't even told my brother and Chelsea the news."

She looked beautiful. And she'd put on a dress.

For him? He was used to seeing Lucy dressed casually, in jeans or shorts. He couldn't remember the last time he'd seen her in a dress. But he liked it.

"You look nice," he said.

"Thank you. But don't change the subject, please. Where did this cradle come from?"

Zane's gaze fell to the little bed next to him. "It was mine, and then Ian used it when he was born. My mom couldn't bear to throw anything away. She was such a pack rat. I used to tease her about that all the time. She used to say, 'You never know when something will come in handy.' I found it in the attic yesterday when I was packing up her place. It's old, but it's in pretty good shape. Sturdy. But if you don't want it, I can give it to the shelter in Dallas. They can always use things like this."

Lucy's face softened. "I do want it. Thank you. It's just that I need to tell Ethan and Chelsea before I start setting up a nursery." Her shoulders rose, then fell. "I hadn't even thought about that until now."

She puffed out her cheeks and blew out her breath. She looked nervous and small, standing there contemplating the task. He hated that she was still thinking she had to go through this alone. What did he have to do to make her see she didn't?

"We'll tell them together," he said. "Whenever you're ready."

While Lucy appeared to be weighing the suggestion, he was formulating all the reasons she shouldn't do this alone.

"We need to set the tone. I'm a grown woman. It's my life, but if we act like this is something shameful, then Ethan will be upset. Really, it's not his call to be upset." She sounded like she was trying to convince herself. "If you want us to tell them together, maybe we can have them over for dinner one night soon. But it's your face Ethan will wreck when he finds out."

The thought had crossed Zane's mind more than once. He and Ethan had been good friends since they were kids. There was a strong possibility that Ethan might take issue with him sleeping with his little sister, but they were all adults now. He was standing by Lucy. She was right—it really wasn't Ethan's business to render an opinion on the situation.

Despite how Lucy might have idolized her big brother, Ethan wasn't perfect. He'd faced his own demons. He would probably understand better than they were anticipating. Maybe they should give the guy more credit.

For a moment Zane grappled with the feeling that he had let Lucy down. That he hadn't protected her. Maybe it would serve him right if Ethan messed up his face.

"I can handle Ethan," he said. "Don't worry about my face."

She reached out and cupped his face in her palm. "But it's such a nice face."

Their gazes locked and this time he found himself grappling with a feeling similar to the one that had done them in that night. The sound of a thunderclap off in the distance broke the spell.

"We'd better get downtown if we are going to beat the rain," he said.

Her hand fell and she took a step back. "I didn't realize it was supposed to rain."

"Just another summer shower. Are you ready to go?"

"Sure, just let me grab my purse."

Lucy returned a minute later with her handbag, but the rain was already starting to fall in fat drops, which were pinging on the front windows and splattering on the porch.

"It's really coming down out there," she said.

She set her small leather purse on the table in the hallway and opened the door. The rain was blowing so hard it was slanting sideways. She turned back to him. "Do you really want to go out in this?"

He shrugged. "Not particularly, but I will if you want to."

She shook her head.

"What's the matter, sugar?" he teased. "You afraid you'll melt?"

She raised her right brow at the comment. "Something like that, because you know I'm so sweet. But don't call me sugar, honey."

He laughed. He loved her sass and the way she could poke fun at herself. He loved the way they bantered. He'd never had that with anyone else. He just wished he could love her the way she deserved to be loved. He didn't need to get ice cream and walk around downtown to know that Lucy Campbell was a good catch for the right man.

"I have an idea," she said. "I have some Rocky Road in the freezer. Let's improvise and eat our ice cream on the porch and listen to the rain. We can sit on the swing. How does that sound?"

It sounded fabulous. Actually, given the choice, he would choose the sanctuary of the rain and the porch swing and Lucy over the curious glances they were bound to get as they ate ice cream as they strolled around downtown together.

Five minutes later, they were seated on the swing with bowls of Rocky Road. She'd taken off her boots and he noticed that her toenails were painted a pale shade of pink. The rain nipped at their feet as they gently swung back and forth and enjoyed the refreshing treat. It hit the spot and took the edge off the humidity, which had been elevated by the sudden summer storm. It was cozy sitting there with her. The white wicker swing, with its cushioned cover and decorative pillows, was just big enough for the two of them, forcing them to sit a little closer than they might have if they had more room. It was nice.

He liked the feel of their thighs touching. He could smell her perfume—something light and floral that tempted him to move in a little closer. So he distracted himself by focusing on the view of the barn about fifty yards away, the gravel road that led to the house where he'd grown up and the fenced-off pastureland beyond that.

Lucy hadn't grown up in this house—her grandparents had lived here. She'd spent a lot of time here and in the barn that was now her business, and she'd inherited the land after her parents' death several years ago. Ethan and their brother, Jude, had inherited equally valued parcels of land. Ethan's was smaller but had the stables from which he ran his horse-breeding business. Several decades ago, his family's ranch had been one of the most successful in the area, but they'd run into financial hardship when alcoholism had gotten the best of Donovan Campbell. For a while it appeared that Ethan might fall down the same slippery slope after his parents' death and the end of his first marriage, but after some soul searching, he had pulled himself up from rock bottom and had set the Triple C Ranch back on the road to profitability.

He was not only a friend but was also an inspiration to Zane, who understood the heartbreak of failed marriage and disappointment of broken dreams. Zane looked up to Ethan, who had managed to not just come out the other side but had emerged on top of life, with his pending marriage and his thriving business.

Lucy had done well for herself, too—after some initial time spent finding herself, she now had the world by the tail. Zane stole a glance at her sitting next to him, looking pretty in her yellow dress.

She loved him. She could have any man she wanted and certainly deserved better than him. But she loved him.

"I'm so happy you could come for dinner tonight," Lucy said to Ethan and Chelsea. "I know it was short notice, but we wanted to cook for you before you get swept away by the wedding. Chels, did you find your shoes yet?"

Chelsea and Ethan stood in Lucy's kitchen, enjoying cheese and crackers that Lucy had set out as an appetizer, as Lucy took the chicken marsala that they were having for dinner out of the oven.

"Actually, I found two pairs. When you have a moment, will you give me your expert opinion as to which you think will work best with the dress? I thought I'd bring both with me when I go in for my final fitting and try them on with the dress."

"Absolutely. I'm sorry I haven't been a very good bridesmaid lately and I know Juliette has been out of town a lot on business. I've been so busy with work lately, too," Lucy said. "I feel like we've left you to your own devices. I'll make it up to you. I promise."

"Don't worry about it," Chelsea said. Her British accent sounded crisp and made everything she said sound *posh*. "You've been fine. No, not just fine. You've been wonderful. Especially considering you've been under the weather so much lately, too. I hope you're not spreading yourself too thin."

Lucy's stomach lurched. She wouldn't allow her

gaze to slant to Zane, who was sitting at the table, having a beer and a completely different conversation with Ethan. Ethan, who'd been sober now for more than three years, was drinking iced tea.

If she looked at Zane, perceptive Chelsea would surely twig that something was up. In fact, she might see right through her and guess why she and Zane had asked her and Ethan to dinner before they'd even had the chance to tell them. Actually, she was surprised Chelsea and Ethan hadn't questioned the invitation in the first place. It wasn't as if she and Zane were in the habit of hosting dinner parties together.

However, if it came up before they were ready to share the news, they'd planned a plausible excuse: as attendants in their wedding, they wanted to spend some time with them before everything got too hectic.

And that was true. But it wasn't the only reason they'd invited them over.

The plan was that they would get through dinner and Zane would break out a bottle of champagne—and sparkling cider for Ethan and Lucy—to have with dessert. They'd toast the upcoming nuptials and their own *good news*. Lucy hoped Chelsea wouldn't pick up on Lucy not drinking wine with dinner.

They'd considered waiting until after Ethan and Chelsea had gotten back from their honeymoon to break the news, because they didn't want to upstage the wedding, but Lucy couldn't take a chance of something slipping. It was best to be direct and set the tone.

She knew that; and everything was going according to the plan, but she was still nervous.

"You're sweet to worry about me, Chelsea, but I'm fine."

Chelsea helped her transport the food to the table in the dining room and they enjoyed some laughs and good conversation over a lovely dinner. As everyone finished their entrées, Lucy grew nervous. But finally, it was time for dessert.

"Zane, will you help me in the kitchen?" Lucy asked.

Chelsea started to stand. "Why don't you stay here and talk to Ethan? I can help you, Lucy."

Chelsea came from a family with a lot of money, and in their posh English estates they probably had a fleet of servants the likes of one might see on *Downton Abbey.* While her offer to help was sincere, living like a commoner—clearing the table and waiting on Ethan hand and foot—was still a novelty to her. If Lucy hadn't been so nervous, she might have laughed silently to herself at the thought of how fast that novelty would wear off once Chelsea was married.

"Oh, Chels, I do appreciate your offer. However, Zane brought the dessert—it's one of Mrs. Anthony's Black Forest cakes. You know she can never resist the opportunity to bake for him. She brings him goodies at least once a month. This month's offering just happened to come at the perfect time for our dinner party. But I will let him do the honors of serving it."

Zane was already on his feet and standing beside Lucy before Chelsea could insist, and the two of them disappeared into the kitchen.

Once they were out of earshot, Lucy asked, "Are you ready for this?"

"I am," he said. "But you look like you're ready to swallow your tongue, you look so nervous."

Lucy shrugged and took four champagne flutes down from one of the kitchen cabinets. Zane's eyebrows arched. "Four? You're not imbibing, are you?"

Lucy shook her head. "I will pour Ethan and myself a glass of sparkling cider, since he won't be drinking, either. I figured it would look very fishy if I walked in with only two glasses."

Zane nodded. "Are you still sure you don't want me to do the talking?"

For a moment, Lucy actually considered it. She obviously looked as nervous as she felt. Maybe it would be a good idea to let Zane take the lead, but then again, she knew what she wanted to say. She would probably be the better of the two of them at keeping the announcement light but to the point.

She shook her head. "No—thanks, though. I've got this. But you can pour yourself and Chelsea a glass of champagne while I open the sparkling cider. And then would you please take the cake into the dining room. I set out some dessert plates on the buffet behind the table."

Zane did as she asked, and before he left the kitchen, he leaned in and gave her a quick peck on the lips. It startled her and a little gasp escaped before she could help herself.

"What was that for?" she asked.

"It was for good luck. Even though we won't need it. We got this. Remember what you kept saying to me—we set the tone. We are not two sixteen-year-olds who are in trouble."

She wanted to ask him why it felt like they were, but she could still feel his kiss—quick as it was—on her lips, and it had bolstered her. It calmed her nerves.

"Right," she said. "We set the tone."

He nodded, one resolute nod, then he flashed that charismatic smile of his that had always made her feel weak in the knees, before he and the cake disappeared from the kitchen. With that, and with the phantom feel of his kiss still on her lips, she knew everything was going to be okay. *Eventually.*

When all the glasses were full and resting on the tray, the cider appeared to be the same light amber color as the bubbly. Unless her brother or Chelsea took a drink from her flute, they would never be the wiser that she wasn't drinking champagne. Of course, they would know soon enough, but at least Lucy would be able to settle in and gather her wits before she broke the news.

"Okay, it's now or never," she whispered to herself. Actually, *never* wasn't an option. She picked up the tray and carried it into the dining room.

"What's this?" Chelsea asked.

"I thought the occasion called for a toast. I have sparkling apple juice for you, my dear brother. And champagne for you, my sweet sister-in-law-to-be." She set the respective flutes in front of each of them and placed one with champagne at Zane's place setting. He served the cake.

"This looks delicious," said Ethan.

"I'm sure Mrs. Anthony made it with an extra dose of love," Lucy teased. Zane waggled his brows as he set the last plate at his place and took a seat.

Lucy and Zane exchanged one last fortifying glance before they lifted their glasses and he said, "A toast to you and your upcoming wedding." They all leaned in and clinked glasses.

Then Lucy said, "And a toast to Zane and me and baby makes three."

Lucy flashed her most brilliant smile as she and Zane clinked champagne flutes, but Chelsea and Ethan sat there with raised glasses and confused looks on their faces.

"What did you just say?" Ethan asked.

Lucy laughed as if she had just shared the news that she had won the megaball lotto jackpot. "I said that we're having a baby. Isn't that wonderful? We are so excited."

Okay, maybe that was stretching it a little bit—

actually, they were petrified—but no one needed to know any different.

The silence was deafening, but finally Chelsea broke the ice.

"Really? Congratulations! I didn't even realize you two were dating. Then again, everyone knows you're crazy about each other. I mean, it's been obvious to me since the moment I first saw you together."

Chelsea shrugged and raised her champagne flute for another go at the toast. Lucy and Zane clinked their glasses to hers, but Ethan sat stock-still, staring at his hands.

"It was that obvious that we're crazy for each other?" Zane asked.

A bubble of nervous laughter escaped Lucy's throat like a hiccup. What was he doing, pretending to be besotted? Probably just trying to lighten the mood—and be convincing. Maybe he was still thinking about the quip she'd made about Ethan messing up his face.

Of course, there were different kinds of "crazy for each other." Their particular brand was that they couldn't keep their hands off each other. Or at least they couldn't help themselves that night. And she could've sworn the other night, when their date had been spontaneously moved to the front porch, that if she'd just leaned in the slightest way, Zane would've kissed her.

But maybe that was just a by-product of the good-luck peck on the lips he'd given her in the kitchen… Or wishful thinking.

She hadn't leaned and he hadn't kissed her the other night. But he'd kissed her just a few minutes ago.

"What are your plans?" Ethan finally spoke and he didn't sound happy. "What does this mean?"

Zane lifted his chin and stared Ethan squarely in the eyes. "What it means is that Lucy and I are going to have a baby."

Chapter Six

The next morning, Lucy looked up from her desk at the sound of someone rapping at her office door.

"Got a few minutes?" Ethan stood in the threshold. Judging by the look on his face, he was trying extra hard not to look grim.

"I always have time for my big brother," Lucy said. "Come in and have a seat. Have you had breakfast? Would you like something to drink?"

Just as he was trying not to look upset, she could feel herself going overboard being cheery and nice.

His hands were clasped in front of him and he shifted from one foot to the other, but he hadn't budged from the door. "No, I'm fine, Lucy, thanks."

She bit the insides of her cheeks to keep herself

from rambling on any more, but after a good minute passed when all they'd done was stare at each other, and he was still rooted to the spot, she finally broke the silence.

"Are you going to come in or are you just going to stare at me from across the room?"

Ethan cleared his throat, then flattened his mouth into a tight line before he finally said, "Why don't we go for a walk?"

She didn't have any appointments until this afternoon. "Sure, that sounds great."

Actually, it sounded pretty serious, like she was being summoned to the principal's office. She knew him well enough to know he wasn't going to get into anything heavy in her office, where people could walk in right in the middle of everything. Hence, the walk.

Even if she hadn't admitted it to herself before now, on a deeper level she'd known they were due for this talk. Last night, Ethan had remained silent as he'd eaten his dessert. Of course, Chelsea had chatted enough for both of them, asking about due dates—Lucy's obstetrician had said the middle of next March—and about whether or not they were going to find out the baby's sex before the birth. Zane had said yes at the same time that Lucy said no. She'd explained that it was like opening a Christmas gift before Christmas. That had inspired a discussion about what color to paint the nursery—gender-neutral sunny yellow, of course.

All the while, Ethan had sat there silently eating his Black Forest cake. And when he was finished, he'd carried his plate to the kitchen and proclaimed it was time to leave, that he had to do his morning rounds of the ranch early and then he had an early meeting. It was the most he'd said since the toast.

It was a good thing that they were getting this talk over with now rather than letting the awkwardness stretch on. Her gratitude that he'd made the first move toward that end overrode her nervousness at his disapproval.

She locked up her office and the barn's front door. This was something new that she'd been forced to start doing since the feature in *Southern Living* magazine. Even though tours were supposed to be by appointment only, several times a week she entertained people who dropped in. One time she'd gone out for lunch and came back only to discover a large wedding party camped out in her office. They hadn't caused any harm, but it was alarming to find them packed into the room. Her office door had been shut, but not locked, and they'd let themselves in and made themselves at home. That was when it dawned on her that she had the petty-cash box, the business's checkbook and other financial information in her unlocked bottom desk drawer. Anyone could let themselves in and help themselves. It felt like the moment Dorothy discovered she wasn't in Kansas anymore. Since the Campbell Wedding Barn had been lifted up and whirled around by the *South-*

ern Living twister—not that she was complaining—
Lucy had decided it was better to be safe than sorry.

Outside, it was a beautiful summer day. It was a
rare mildly warm day with a clear robin's-egg-blue
sky and a gentle breeze that ruffled the live oaks
and tousled Lucy's hair. Luckily, she had slipped an
elastic band onto her wrist that morning, because it
had been one of the rare instances that her hair was
behaving. But as unpredictable as the weather had
been lately, if the day decided to take a turn toward
hot and humid, she wanted to be prepared to pull her
hair back so that it wasn't on her neck. Maybe it was
just her imagination, but since discovering she was
pregnant, her body temperature was already running
warmer than usual.

Since Ethan had been so good to initiate this talk,
Lucy decided she would be the one to get the ball
rolling by easing into the inevitable conversation.

"How was your meeting this morning?"

It wasn't what he'd come to talk about, she knew
that, but at least it would get the ball rolling.

"Fine. A guy from over at McKinney wanted
to talk about breeding his mare. We'll see where
it goes."

They walked in silence for a few minutes, until
they reached the white post-and-rail fence that ran
between the gravel road that snaked through the
Campbell property and the pastures where Lucy's
land ended and Ethan's began. It wasn't so much
that they needed to define whose land was whose,

as much as it was that Ethan's business dealt with horses and Lucy's dealt solely with people. It was the best way to keep the two separate.

Suddenly, Ethan stopped and turned toward his sister, which forced him to squint into the sun. "Do I need to get the shotgun and make an honest man out of Zane?"

Lucy's eyes grew wide. She shook her head vigorously. "No, Ethan. No shotgun needed." She knew he was speaking figuratively. She hoped. Of course he was.

"Zane asked me to marry him."

A look of relief passed over Ethan's face. "Why didn't you say so? When's the wedding?"

"The only wedding on the books is yours and Chelsea's. Zane and I are not getting married."

"Why not? He proposed and all."

"I said no because I don't want to get married."

Ethan's face screwed up like he didn't understand a word she was saying. "But you're pregnant. Why don't you want to get married? Don't you think you should?"

"When did you become so old-fashioned, Ethan? No, I don't think we should get married. Zane proposed—if you can even call it that. It really wasn't a proposal as much as a very unromantic declaration that he had decided we should get married. I told him I had decided we would do no such thing. It's not what I want."

Ethan put his hands on his hips. "Lucy, you are

going to have a baby. You and Zane are going to be parents. When you got pregnant, you forfeited your right to fanciful notions about princes and princesses and saying no to a marriage proposal because the proposal wasn't romantic enough. You need to grow up."

"I said no because Zane doesn't love me. Okay? Are you happy now?"

"Lucy, what the hell are you doing messing around with a guy who doesn't love you? You should have more self-respect than that."

Her mouth fell open and she saw red. "That is none of your business, Ethan. I'm sure you slept with plenty of women you didn't love after you and Molly broke up and before you met Chelsea. And I'm sure you wouldn't be having this conversation with Jude. I really thought you were more evolved than to perpetuate double standards. But the bottom line is, you are not my father and you have no business imposing your hang-ups on me."

"And what do you think our father would be saying to you if he was here right now?"

Lucy's mouth fell open. Tears stung her eyes. That was a low blow.

"That's not fair, Ethan. Daddy isn't here anymore and it's hurtful for you to throw that at me right now." She turned to walk back to her office, because right now she needed to be as far away from her brother as she could get.

"Lucy, stop. Come back. Please."

She stopped and whirled around to face him. "I appreciate your concern, but I am a grown woman with a thriving business that allows me to support myself. I'm not marrying Zane and I am not asking for your blessing. So, you can just get over it."

As her tears started to fall, she turned around and started toward the barn, keeping a brisk pace and not looking back. When she was safe inside, she latched the door, went into her office, buried her head in her hands and sobbed.

Having a baby on her own should mean that she was strong and self-sufficient, but it broke her heart that Ethan seemed to be looking at her as his flaky little sister, the one who always managed to mess things up. For a split second she worried that maybe he was right, that maybe she was getting in over her head. After all, this decision wasn't just about her. It involved a tiny little life that hadn't asked to be brought into this situation. This baby wasn't something she could try out and quit like she had so many times in the past when she got bored or dreamed up something shiny and new.

She lifted her head to pull a tissue from her desk drawer, and she caught a glimpse of the sunshine that was streaming in through the skylights along the barn's rooftop. Turning this old ramshackle barn into a place that had become one of the South's premier wedding venues had taken every ounce of everything that she possessed—money, energy, blood, sweat and more than a few tears. It had been her baby, and she hadn't quit on it. Not even when times had gotten tough. She didn't intend to quit on it anytime soon, either.

Even if her brother thought she was a flake, she knew she wasn't. She was having this baby and she didn't need to tie herself to a man who didn't love her in order to make it work, in order to be a good mother. Of course, it would be so much easier if she had her family's support, but if she didn't…

The sound of somebody unlocking the front door had her scrambling to wipe away her tears. She needed to pull herself together. She needed to remember that this was her decision, and if Ethan was going to judge her for it, it was his problem, not hers. But a moment later, her brother was standing in the doorway to her office just as he had when he'd first arrived, before their walk.

"Ethan, we're not having this discussion here. This is my place of business and— No, you know what? For that matter, were not having this discussion anywhere. The discussion's over. You can go back to the stables."

"I'm sorry," he said. That was when she noticed that her big, strong oldest brother actually had tears glistening in his own eyes. "You are absolutely right. That was a sexist, chauvinistic thing for me to say and I'm sorry. Lucy, I only want the best for you. And I guess in some ways I do feel like more of a father to you than a big brother."

In many ways, that was true. After their parents

died, Ethan had come back to Celebration, uprooting him and his ex-wife, Molly, from Chicago to come home and care for her. She'd been only fourteen years old. Their father died the night of the accident. Their mother, who had been left a paraplegic, died a few months later. Rather than relocate her to Chicago, Ethan had moved back so that she could finish high school in Celebration. In the end, his own marriage broke up over the move back to their small hometown. Never once did he blame her or make her feel as if it was her fault.

Maybe she needed to cut him some slack. She wasn't changing her position, but she didn't have to excommunicate him.

"Ethan, I appreciate you saying that." She drew in a deep breath, trying to buy herself some time so she could weigh her words. "It's so important to me to have you on my side because you're important to me."

He shook his head. "You need to know that I am on your side, Lucy. I only want what's best for you. I want you to be happy. I don't want life to be any harder on you than it has to be."

"Then please understand that's exactly why I'm choosing not to marry Zane. We are going to coparent, and we're going to be great at it. He even seems pretty psyched about it. That will work, but tying myself to someone who doesn't love me, to someone who didn't choose to be with me out of love, won't make me happy. In fact, in the end, it will make both of us pretty darn miserable."

She remembered the feeling of Zane's lips on hers last night, she remembered the way their bodies had felt together—how they'd worked so well together. A profound sadness washed over her and she shuddered. She was damned if she did, damned if she didn't. But the most damning part of it would be if she roped Zane into a marriage he didn't really want and the two of them ended up being a new-millennium replay of his parents.

The person who would suffer the most would be their sweet child. Zane, of all people, should understand that after what he'd gone through growing up.

After work, Zane dropped by the hardware store and purchased two gallons of yellow paint called soft banana. He'd spent some time on the internet researching the best shade of yellow for a baby's room and had learned that a yellow that was too bright could make the baby agitated, while a soft, pastel shade had warm, calming effects. When he'd looked through the various color chips in the paint section, soft banana seemed to fit the bill.

He was going to surprise Lucy with it. If she hated it, they could go together and choose another color, but for now, he wasn't sure how many clues she wanted to drop around town—even though shopping for yellow paint together didn't exactly scream "we're having a baby!" it might raise a few eyebrows.

Now that they'd shared the news with Ethan and Chelsea, there was no reason they couldn't get a jump on converting Lucy's spare room into the nursery. Last night when she'd said she wanted to paint the walls yellow, he'd decided to go for it. Get the paint and get to work. Actually, he hoped his proactive approach would prove to Lucy how much he cared about his child—their child. And he hoped Ethan would consider it a sign of his commitment, that he wasn't going to flake out on Lucy and their child. Ethan had been pretty stoic last night after they'd shared the news. Chelsea, God love her, had enough enthusiasm for everyone, but Zane knew that he and Ethan were due a heart-to-heart before too long.

First, he and Lucy needed to figure out what they were going to do. He wasn't pushing her, but he still hadn't given up on the possibility of convincing her to marry him.

He might not believe in love the way she wanted him to, but frankly, he believed some things were more important than a nebulous, fleeting, highly overrated emotion.

He hoped she realized actions spoke louder than words. In this case, he hoped his gesture spoke volumes, filling in the spaces where he simply didn't have the words.

Next, he went to the Campbell property and found Ethan at the Triple C offices.

"Got a minute?" he asked.

It was almost imperceptible, but Zane saw Ethan

stiffen when he looked up from the paperwork on his desk and saw Zane standing there.

They needed to talk this out. Based on what Lucy had told him about Ethan's suggestion of a shotgun wedding, he was taking the news of his sister's pregnancy about the way Zane thought he would.

"Sure. Come in. Shut the door."

The office was small and rustic. Zane sat in one of the empty chairs in front of Ethan's desk.

"Thanks for letting me take my time clearing my mom's stuff out of the bungalow," he said. "I am going to wrap things up this evening. I've dragged it out long enough. It's time."

"We don't have any plans for the house yet. There's no hurry if you need more time."

Ethan was making all the right noises, but Zane could tell that he wasn't himself.

"Thanks, I appreciate that. But that's not the reason I came by."

Ethan nodded, but he didn't say anything. He was staring at a spot over Zane's left shoulder.

"If you want to punch me, go ahead," Zane said.

He was serious.

Unsmiling, Ethan locked gazes with him.

"Yeah, I thought about doing that more than a couple of times."

He was serious, too.

"Okay, how do you want to handle it? Do you want to set up a time, like a duel? Or do you just want to take me out right now?"

Ethan still didn't smile.

"Are you making a joke out of this?"

Zane raked a hand through his hair and then composed his most serious face.

"This isn't a joke to me. It's one of the most serious things that's ever happened to me and that's exactly how I'm treating it. But that's between Lucy and me. I came by as a courtesy to you to let you know that I intend to stand by your sister. I would marry her if she would have me, but that's something she's not so sure about."

Ethan was doodling on the yellow legal pad on his desktop.

"Are you in love with my sister, Zane?"

He had known this was coming. It was a perfectly logical question that a big brother would ask the guy who'd gotten his little sister pregnant.

"With all due respect, that's between Lucy and me."

Ethan let the pen fall from his hand and his gaze nailed Zane to his chair.

"Since you can't give me a straight answer, I'll take that as a no."

Zane should have been prepared for that, but he wasn't. It wasn't that cut-and-dried. He couldn't say he *didn't* love her. He cared about her—

Ethan smirked. "We could fall down a big black hole talking about all the reasons you shouldn't have slept with Lucy if you don't love her. But I know my sister. I know how she feels about you, and I know, deep down, you are a decent guy. *Don't* hurt her, Zane." He spat the word *don't* through gritted teeth. "And don't expect her to tie herself to a guy who doesn't return her feelings."

"I'm not going to hurt her. At least not on purpose."

"Yeah. That's what I'm afraid of," Ethan said. "It usually happens when we don't intend it."

They sat quietly for a few beats as the truth of Ethan's words swirled around them.

Finally, Ethan said, "Thanks for coming to clear the air. I was wondering how long it would take for you to slink in here."

That was better. He sounded more like himself again.

"I don't *slink*," Zane said. "The only one who's going to *slink* anywhere is you when I beat your sorry ass at bowling. Only you would have your bachelor party at the bowling alley."

They talked for a while, about horses and houses, and about how one of the guests at Ethan and Chelsea's wedding was her brother, who would most likely be the next prime minister of the United Kingdom. The security was crazy, but that would be their new normal when it came to Chelsea's family.

Zane was happy things were back to normal with Ethan, but he had to get a move on. The final boxes weren't going to move themselves. He drove his truck away from the offices to the gravel frontage road that led to the bungalow. He hadn't realized it until he was parked in the driveway in front of the house, but by delaying the move out, it had been easier to ignore the fact that his mom was gone. But she was. Putting it off wasn't going to bring her back. So tonight he would wrap it up.

He let himself inside the house. All the blinds were drawn, making the place dark and dank. The cardboard boxes were starting to smell a little musty from being closed up in the humid house all these weeks that Zane couldn't deal. He cranked up the AC, let in some light and got to work. He made himself focus on the task and not think too hard about how the place looked empty and sad without most of his mom's things. It didn't even resemble the home that his mother had worked so hard to make for them. She'd done her best to provide for them. That was why she'd hung on to so much stuff. But in the end, all the *things* she'd accumulated, the stacks of fabric, piles of old patterns, half-finished projects and mounds of sewing supplies he couldn't even identify—the stuff that had made her feel safe, as if she owned a little bit of something in this world— didn't mean a damn thing. None of it had saved her when it mattered. The remnants of her life only served as a reminder to Zane that she'd gotten a raw deal when she trusted Nathaniel Phillips.

Zane was going to do better by his child.

A few hours later, he'd packed the last of her stuff. The boxes were ready to load into the bed of his truck. He'd separated things into four piles: keep, give away, trash and to be determined. The latter pile consisted of things he didn't know what to do with. He'd snapped photos of things Ian might want and sent them to him. He'd ask Lucy about the other stuff. She might want some of it. She and his mom had bonded over crafty things. She might want some of her sewing supplies.

He loaded the last box and went back inside for one more look around. He'd hire Virginia Kelly, who had a cleaning service, to come over and put the final shine on the place. But his work here was done. The only thing he had to contend with was the trash. He started to tie off one of the lone remaining industrial garbage bags, but his well-loved and time-ravaged stuffed bear peeked out of the opening. Zane pulled it out.

He'd loved that thing when he was a child. Rather than a blanket, the bear had been his comfort and best friend. He'd dragged it around everywhere. He'd tossed it because it was too old and threadbare to be of any use to anyone. It wasn't worth saving for the baby, but for some reason, instead of throwing it away, he wanted to share this connection to his past with Lucy.

Suddenly, he was grateful that his mom had kept things like the cradle and his bear. Zane realized that they were not only links to his past, but also links to his mom. She hadn't just managed to give Ian and him a good, loving upbringing, but, even after she was gone, through the things she'd chosen to keep, she'd helped him realize that maybe his past did hold some memories worth hanging on to. For a melancholy moment, he wished Dorothy could be there to hold her first grandchild the way she'd tenderly held him when he'd needed her, but she wasn't here. At least not in the flesh, but he felt her presence all around him like a hug—just when he needed it. Just like she'd always done.

Zane was filled with the overwhelming realization that the best way he could honor his mother was by being a good father to his own child. By being more like her and not like his own father.

As he stared down at the ugly stained bear in his hands, a quiet calm came over him. Maybe it was all in how he looked at life. From one angle, the bear, which had once been snowy white, but was now a funky tea-stained yellow brown, looked like trash. From another perspective, it represented the comfort of his past.

Maybe he could apply the same lens to love. He knew that was what his mom would tell him.

He closed his eyes, stood there still in the empty house and tried to imagine himself in love with Lucy.

While it didn't crash over him like a breaking wave or envelop him like the sticky Texas humidity, something was there—like a swell in the ocean or the feel of a warm spring breeze. But where he turned a corner was when he looked at it from the opposite perspective and tried to imagine his life without Lucy and their child. That was the biggest shift. He knew without a doubt he needed them in his life.

He tied up the trash, tucked the one-eyed teddy bear under his arm and let himself out. As he was locking up, he heard the crunch of tires on the gravel drive behind him. It was just getting dark. Through the inky twilight haze, he could see a big black pickup parking next to his own truck. The windows were tinted, and the way the headlights shone in his eyes, he couldn't readily recognize the driver. But soon enough the door opened and Nathaniel Phillips unfolded his lanky body as he exited the truck's cab.

Zane's ire prickled. His mouth flattened into a hard line. He cursed under his breath but kept his attention trained on the house door until he was sure it was locked. Then his fingers reflexively fisted into his palms.

What the hell does he want?

Zane was certain he'd made it perfectly clear where they stood when the bastard had the audacity to show up at Dorothy's funeral. The guy couldn't have been bothered to come around for the past twenty-five years. Now the jackass seemed to turn up around every corner.

Zane stood there stoically. He would let Nathaniel speak first. Or better yet he could turn around and get back in that fancy Ford F-150—Zane could see now that he wasn't blinded by the headlights—and drive off a cliff, for all he cared.

Those trucks didn't come cheap. The bastard must

be doing all right for himself. Of course, he could never spare a penny for them. He lived in Dallas now. Or at least that was the last address that Zane knew of. He hadn't cared to keep track of him over the years.

"Son." Nathaniel hesitated for a minute. "I saw your truck from the highway as I was passing by."

It was on the tip of Zane's tongue to tell him to never call him *son* again. He had three sons with Marianne Crawford—the three kids he'd bothered to take responsibility for and raise. Wasn't that enough? Why was he suddenly coming around now?

"What do you want, Nathaniel? I was just leaving." Zane took a step toward his own truck, but Nathaniel moved at the same time, blocking the way. It wasn't an aggressive move, but it put Zane on alert.

As a general rule, Zane wasn't a violent person. He didn't get in bar fights, he thought road rage was ridiculous—everyone had places to go—and he didn't believe beating someone's ass made him more of a man. Still, Nathaniel seemed to bring out the worst in him, because suddenly all he wanted to do was pound the sorry excuse for a man who was standing in his way.

"Move," Zane said through gritted teeth.

Nathaniel seemed to shrink, but he didn't budge. "I stopped here to ask you if you'd have dinner with me sometime."

Zane laughed in his face. "Why would I want to do that?"

Nathaniel closed his eyes for a moment, and Zane took the opportunity to scoot by him. But Nathaniel must've sensed the movement, because he opened his eyes and turned toward Zane.

"I know I've never been much of a father to you," he said. "And I'm sorry about that. If you would let me, I'd like to try to make it up to you."

The words pierced Zane like arrows. They stung on impact but left him numb. It made no sense. After all these years, now that Dorothy was gone…now that Nathaniel was ready, he thought he could come around and everything would be fine?

Zane didn't know whether he wanted to punch the guy or laugh in his face.

No, he didn't deserve his anger. It was too good for him. He didn't deserve any of Zane's energy. Anger took energy. Anger meant he cared. Zane wanted to give the bastard exactly what he deserved: absolutely nothing.

Even so, all kinds of thoughts—all of the frustration and hurt and things he'd wanted to say to Nathaniel over the decades that the man had turned his back on Dorothy, Ian and himself—got log-jammed in his throat. Zane knew if he didn't get in his truck right now and drive away, those words were going to organize themselves and he was going to unload them all over Nathaniel Phillips. He had never been a father to him. What the hell made him think he could come blundering back now?

"My mother worked herself into an early grave

because you wanted nothing to do with us when we needed you." His voice was calm and even, void of emotion. "You made her sell the ranch that had been in her family for generations when you decided you didn't want to hang around anymore. You thought you deserved half so you could take care of your other family with Marianne. We got by without you then. What makes you think that you can make it up to me now?"

Nathaniel opened his mouth to say something, but the words were lost when Zane got into the cab of his truck. He tossed the sorry-looking stuffed bear into the backseat and slammed the door. As he pulled away, he glanced in the rearview mirror only once and he saw Nathaniel's silhouette illuminated by the taillights of Zane's truck. His father looked like the sorry man he was.

Zane probably should've gone home, because he wasn't in a very good head space. In fact, he felt like he needed to punch a wall. But his instincts led him to Lucy. Suddenly, she felt like the only tangible thing of substance in his miserable life.

He didn't blame her for not wanting to marry him. She deserved so much more than his offering of soft-banana paint and a stained, threadbare stuffed animal.

After seeing Nathaniel and remembering all the years of heartbreak he'd put Dorothy through and all the broken promises he'd dished out to Ian and him, was it any wonder he had no idea what love was?

Nathaniel Phillips withheld a lot from him when he was growing up, but he'd be damned if he was going to let the bastard cost him his future. For the first time in a long time he knew the only future he wanted was with Lucy and his child.

He was tired of words and lame promises. No, he had to let his actions speak for themselves.

Lucy's red Toyota sat beside the house when he arrived. He parked next to it, then stomped up the front porch steps and pounded on the door.

When she answered, she looked surprised. "Zane—"

But he didn't give her the chance to say anything else, because he pulled her into his arms and covered her mouth with his. As her lips opened under his, passion consumed him. In that moment, he wanted to walk her backward right into the bedroom and make love to her. Instead, he deepened the kiss and pulled her even tighter against him.

He wasn't sure how long they stayed like that, but when they came up for air, Lucy looked dazed. Her hand flew up to her kiss-swollen lips.

"What was that for?" she asked. "I mean, I loved it, but… Zane? What's going on?"

He wasn't quite sure what to say, how to tell her about his epiphany at the house and that he'd just seen his father and the combination of the two encounters had caused his entire life to flash before his eyes. That he didn't want to be like Nathaniel Phillips. That if she would have him, he would never hurt her.

"I realized today that I don't want to lose you."

"You did?" She took his hand and pulled him inside, shutting the door behind them. She looked cute in the denim shorts and red blouse she was wearing. More than cute, actually. She looked sexy as hell. How had he been so blind all these years?

"And what exactly inspired this epiphany?" she asked.

He weighed his words and thought about what to say. Telling the truth was best, but it was messy. It contained too much baggage and he was tired of lugging it around. "It doesn't matter. I know I'm not any good at this love thing, but if you'll give me a chance, I can promise you that I will never let you down. What do you say, Lucy? Will you give me a chance?"

Chapter Seven

What was Lucy supposed to do? The love of her life had asked her to give him a chance.

After he'd kissed her senseless, every bit of resolve she had cobbled into place systematically unraveled, as if he had pulled a single thread and left her guard lying in a tangled heap at her feet.

Of course she'd give him a chance. As if she even had a choice in the matter. A girl could only be so strong.

However, *a chance* didn't necessarily mean she'd marry him. Not yet, anyway. Maybe not ever. She didn't know. She was still reeling from the force of that kiss. Her lips were still tingling.

All she knew right now was that Ethan and Chelsea needed to get married first. It wasn't a competition, of course, but if Lucy had learned one thing since opening the Campbell Wedding Barn, it was that every bride, no matter how humble, deserved to be a princess for a day. Lucy wasn't going to do anything to upstage Chelsea on her big day.

Lucy knew that the truth of the matter was if she and Zane ran off and got married—or even hinted that they were considering it—the focus of the entire town would turn to them and how little Lucy Campbell had run off and married Celebration's most eligible bachelor. People would speculate about the reason—and they'd be right.

So, no, Lucy wasn't going to even consider anything until after her brother and Chelsea had tied the knot.

That was fine. After *the kiss*, Zane had presented her with two gallons of paint—not just any paint, but the perfect shade of yellow for their baby's nursery. In some ways, this gesture made her even more inclined to entertain the thought of marrying him. It had made her really ponder—what exactly was the meaning of love? How was the best way to declare love? Anyone could say those three little words. He could've very well told her exactly what she wanted to hear and she would've fallen for it. Because she had already fallen for him.

But in the Zane fairy tale in her mind, his going to the trouble of finding the perfect shade of yellow was almost metaphorical to Prince Charming searching the kingdom for the woman whose foot fit the glass slipper.

Well, sort of… It had seemed a bit more romantic as it came to her in a rush. Practically speaking, she could use two gallons of the perfect shade of yellow much more than she could use a glass slipper.

Or had Cinderella ended up with a matching pair? If so, why did everything but the glass slippers revert to their original state at the stroke of midnight? And if only a single slipper remained… Oh, who cared? Hadn't fairy-tale standards caused her more trouble than they were worth? And who needed glass slippers anyway, when the man of her dreams gave her a whole heck of a lot more than lip service?

Zane had come through. He had been there for her. Shouldn't the little gestures like the cradle and the thought he'd put into the perfect shade of paint and that ragged, one-eyed teddy bear prove that he was in this? That he was committed? If this wasn't love, what was?

If only she could exorcise the demon that kept saying, "Everything is fine now, but what if, like Cinderella, everything does evaporate at the stroke of midnight?" In this case, midnight would happen if Zane met another woman who ended up being the love of his life and he fell head over heels in love.

It had happened to his own father with Marianne—though Lucy would never insult Zane by showing him that parallel.

That would be her midnight; it would be the darkest night of her soul.

And the earth would end someday and she might walk outside and get hit by a car smack-dab in the middle of the crosswalk. Nothing was guaranteed. Not even tomorrow. The angel on her shoulder began to override the demon: what if Zane never fell in love with anyone else and she had wasted her chance with him? What if this *was* Zane in love?

As they worked side-by-side, painting their baby's nursery soft banana, Lucy began to ignore her doubts. Not only did she let down her guard, but she also let herself hope and imagine what it would be like to become Mrs. Zane Phillips and have a family with the man she loved.

Lucy was in the middle of finalizing the seating configuration for Ethan and Chelsea's wedding ceremony when a text came through from Zane.

Are you up for a lunch break?

She wasn't, really, because she was already behind the eight ball with the seating plans. Two hours ago, Chelsea had asked if they had room to add twenty-five more people. Space was already tight, but Lucy told her she would get creative and see what she could do. She was supposed to meet with Lauren Walters, the assistant she hired on an as-needed basis to help with larger events. She'd planned on

working through lunch to have the seating arrangements ready for the meeting. But now she was suddenly famished. Funny how that always seemed to
happen when Zane called.

She replied to Zane. What did you have in mind?

Actually, I'm right outside. You keep this place
locked up like a prison. Will you let me in?

Are you equating my wedding venue to a prison?

A moment passed without a reply and Lucy
wished she'd included some kind of emoticon to in-
dicate she was kidding. Surely, he realized she was
kidding? Didn't he?

And then he texted back. I brought subs and
chips.

So much for trying to joke around through the
magical medium of texting. She should know better.
Sometimes humor got lost over the waves. She got
up from her desk and opened the barn's front door.
There stood Zane. Her first glimpse of him after
spending time apart always knocked the air out of
her for an instant—in the very best way—and this
was no exception.

"Hi," she said. "Are you here to turn yourself in?"

He laughed. Sort of. Had something in the double meaning of equating marriage to prison struck
a nerve? Because his sense of humor was notably
absent.

"Sure," he said.

"Good, because I deal in standard-issue ball and chains. But you can bond out of jail with the payment of one sub sandwich and a bag of chips."

He held up the white paper sack. "Sounds like a deal."

That was more like it.

Lucy motioned for Zane to follow her into the kitchen. He unwrapped the sandwiches and set them on the paper that they came in while she poured them each a glass of iced tea and put a lemon wedge on the rim of each glass.

"You look nice," he said, giving her an approving once-over.

She was wearing jeans and a simple white lace blouse. Casual and comfortable, but she had a jacket hanging on the back of her door to dress up her look if a potential client came by.

"Thanks, cowboy. You don't look so bad yourself."

Zane always looked sexy no matter what he was wearing. Today, his plain khaki green T-shirt brought out the hazel flecks in his brown eyes. She could lose herself in those eyes, she thought as she waited for him to look up and catch her staring. She wanted him to catch her, wanted to flirt with him and turn the flirting into kissing, but he was too busy contemplating his sandwich.

She resisted the urge to fill the silence by asking him if everything was all right. They ate without talking for a while. Something felt a little bit off. Lucy couldn't put her finger on it, but something was definitely weird. Then again, it was probably her. She was tired and short on time, which was probably making her a little anxious. She needed to cool her jets.

After all, he was the one who had surprised her by showing up with lunch, just when she needed it. She was hungrier than she'd realized. This was probably just a blood-sugar episode. Or simple overthinking.

If things were to work out between the two of them, she could not melt into a heap of self-doubt at his every quiet mood. He was human—he was allowed to have good days and bad days, vocal days and days when he just needed to turn inside. The best relationships were the ones where the couples could be equally happy interacting and spending quiet moments side by side in companionable silence. She was going to have to become best friends with her self-confidence. All her life, she'd never been short on self-confidence. Lately, she was needing to dig deep and get reacquainted with it. This off-kilter feeling, this sensation of spinning out of control and not knowing where she was going to land when she stopped, was so uncomfortable.

But she needed to get her bearings so she could land on her feet.

She pondered this as she ate her sandwich. Zane had already finished and was cleaning up his trash. He took his glass to the sink, washed and dried it.

"Thanks for bringing lunch," she said. "I needed a break more than I realized." She glanced at her watch. "Lauren should be here in a few minutes to go over the details of Ethan and Chelsea's wedding. I'm counting on her, since Juliette and I will both be part of the wedding party." She shook her head. "Maybe I should've brought someone else in to help Lauren, given all the added security."

"It's not like you won't be right here," he said over his shoulder. "Plus, as hard as you and Juliette have been working on this, it could probably run itself."

"If only. Events only look effortless when someone is doing a darn good job of steering the ship behind the scenes."

Zane walked back to the kitchen island and sat down. Resting his forearms on his thighs, he looked at her for a moment. She could virtually see the wheels turning in his head.

"What is it? Are you okay? You've been really quiet." The look on his face didn't do much to make her feel better.

"I have some news," he said, and she had a sinking feeling she wasn't going to love what he had to say. As she swallowed the last bite of her sandwich, it stuck in her throat. She had to wash it down with a gulp of iced tea.

"Good news, I hope."

He gave her a half smile and a one-shoulder shrug. "Depends on how you look at it."

Silence stretched between them until she couldn't stand it anymore.

"Are you going to tell me or do I have to guess?"

"I heard back from Hidden Rock in Ocala."

"Oh." She did her best to put a smile in her voice and on her face, one that reached her eyes, because she should be happy for him. She wanted to be happy for him.

But the truth was she was scared to death. What did this mean?

Things had just started going so well she'd actually forgotten about the Ocala possibility. Of course, it had lived somewhere in the corner of her subconscious. She had to admit that she'd hoped the job had lost its shine for him, and that maybe, just maybe, after all that had happened, he'd decided that he wanted to stay in Celebration.

"Did they offer you the job?" She held her breath as she waited for his answer.

"Not exactly," he said. "They want me to come out again. So they can show me the ropes. They want to introduce me to the rest of the staff and talk specifics—probably negotiate salary and such."

"So, basically, it's imminent? They're going to offer you the job, Zane. I mean, they wouldn't bring you all the way back out and introduce you around there if it wasn't a strong possibility, right?"

"I don't know. Maybe?"

She arched a brow at him and he shifted in his seat and ran a hand through his unruly hair.

"Probably," he said.

"I know how much you want this job." It hurt her heart to acknowledge that. But she had to.

"Of course." His eyes flashed and then in an instant a look of unfathomable realization commandeered his expression as his gaze dropped to Lucy's belly. "But things have changed. I can't leave. I probably should tell them I can't take the job."

Their lives flashed before Lucy's eyes. This was how the end would begin. He would turn down his dream job. For a while he would pretend it didn't matter. Maybe he'd even convince himself it didn't. He'd keep working at Bridgemont, and resentment would take root and grow inside him, until it spread like kudzu and strangled the life out of them and anything that might resemble a relationship.

"Why would you do that?" she asked, working so hard to keep her voice from breaking.

"Really?" His smile was a challenge.

"Zane, I'm serious. You are not turning down a job because of me. Don't put that on me."

"Did I say I blamed you? Because I don't remember mentioning your name."

He flashed that lopsided smile and she could tell he was trying not to let the conversation devolve into a fight, trying to pretend as if this was no big deal, but his eyes gave him away.

"I think we're getting a little bit ahead of ourselves here. They haven't officially offered me the job. You're trying to ship me off already." There was that teasing smile again. "I guess I never considered the fact that you might want to get rid of me."

"Then who would bring me lunch on those days when I didn't even realize I needed it?" she said.

He reached out and toyed with a strand of her hair. "I imagine there would be someone who would be eager to take my place."

Take my place.

His place.

"No one could ever take your place." She'd said the words before she could stop herself and immediately wished she could reel them back in. He reached out and took her hand, brought it to his lips and kissed it.

"Come with me, Luce."

She shook her head, a little dazed. "You know I can't do that." She gestured around her. "Zane, my life is here. I have my business. My family is here."

"You don't have to give it up. You could get Lauren to run it for you—at least for a while. I mean, when you're out on maternity leave."

His words swirled around her. The mere thought of leaving everything she'd worked so hard to build made her feel light-headed. She couldn't even respond.

"You've done a great job with the Campbell Wedding Barn. Maybe you could branch out and do something similar in Florida. Aren't you ready for a new challenge? A chance to try something new? Or here's a thought—you and Juliette have been working so closely together. Have you ever considered merging your businesses? If not Lauren, maybe Juliette could manage the Texas location while you expand the operation in Ocala. I mean, I'm just thinking out loud, but what do you think? You and Juliette are both entrepreneurs. You're great at things like that."

She shook her head. Her heart was pounding and she felt like she was on the verge of tears. "I think Juliette should be part of that conversation before we start making business decisions for her."

"I know, I said I'm just thinking out loud."

She tried to swallow her emotions and see it from his point of view. It was a good idea in theory. Taking a leap of faith and following him to Ocala. It could be an adventure…or a disaster.

Even so, a merger with Juliette was a tall order.

"If Juliette is here managing the barn, who will tend to her business? She travels a lot. I'm sure she wouldn't be too keen about the idea of giving up everything she's built just to accommodate us."

"Okay, I see your point, but that's where Lauren could come in. You're going to have to take some time off when the baby comes. You're going to need someone to cover for you while you're on maternity leave."

She blinked. Her head swam at the thought. She hadn't even thought that far ahead. She was still getting use to the idea of being pregnant. Still trying to figure out exactly how she and Zane fit into each other's lives. Because just when she thought she had it figured out, everything changed. His pending offer for the job in Ocala was case in point.

"I don't know, Zane. I haven't gotten there yet. All I know is I don't want you to turn down this job for me."

He inhaled sharply and then blew out the breath. It wasn't an impatient sound—it seemed more like a nervous gesture. "All I'm asking is for you to think about it. We don't have to make any decisions right now."

She brushed some sandwich crumbs into a small pile with her finger.

"Good, because right now I'm on overload with all the last-minute details for Ethan and Chelsea's wedding. My head is too full."

So was her heart.

He nodded and unfolded his tall body from the chrome bar stool. "I understand. I do. I get it. I know this is a lot to spring on you all at once. Are you finished with your lunch?"

She nodded and he gathered up her trash. He was good to her in little ways like that. Small, kind gestures that she was getting used to.

"I have to get back to work," he said. "You don't have to answer me now. Not until after your brother's wedding. Just promise me you'll give it some thought. Okay?"

"You're going after the wedding?"

"Yeah. Last time I checked, I was standing up with Ethan."

"When he and I talked, he asked if he needed to get out the shotgun."

"He mentioned that." He smiled. "Maybe that's not a bad idea. Would it convince you to marry me?"

With his job offer pending, getting married seemed like the easy part now. The difficult choice was whether or not to leave everything behind and relocate.

"Are you going to tell him about Ocala?" she asked.

He crossed his arms over his chest and she was distracted by the way his biceps bunched, testing the limit of his T-shirt sleeves. She wanted to touch him. What would he do if she did? They were still in that strange limbo land—together...sort of. Lovers... once. Parents...almost. In love...one of them was.

It hit her that *if* they got married, she had no idea what kind of a marriage they'd have. Would they be lovers? If not—if he'd made his original just-friends mandate because he didn't desire her but didn't want to hurt her feelings—what was the postmarriage plan?

The fact that she even had to wonder about these things reminded her of what an emotionally precarious situation this was. She wasn't going to have an open marriage, but she wasn't okay with the thought of living like a nun for the rest of her life, either.

That song from the '80s that talked about looking at the menu but not being able to eat came to mind. She'd add it to her Zane playlist.

"I'm not going to tell anyone yet," he said. "Not until we have a plan."

"Right now, the plan is that we're having a baby."

He nodded. "What if you visit Ocala with me when I go?"

Her heart wanted to go in the worst—and best—way. Her heart wanted to follow him to the ends of the earth. But the logical part of her warned that it was an impossible situation.

"You could see the town. Try it on for size and see if it fits. See what you think. Because maybe if we got away from Celebration, we could figure out if we could be happy there together."

And that was the crux of the matter. They had no idea if they could be happy together in the long run. In Ocala, here or anywhere.

Wasn't it a telltale sign that they still wanted such different things? He couldn't wait to get out of town, while her entire life was right here.

At least for now, she thought as he kissed her on the cheek and walked out the door.

Chapter Eight

The day of Ethan and Chelsea's wedding dawned bright and beautiful.

Chelsea's immediate family—her father, the Earl of Downing; her mother, the countess; two brothers, Thomas, the probable future UK prime minister, and Niles, a doctor; her sister, Victoria, a fashion designer, who had created Chelsea's gown—had all arrived from the United Kingdom with all of the security required by a family of nobility with political ties.

The entourage made the Campbell family look low maintenance by comparison.

Jude, Ethan and Lucy's brother, had managed to find his way back to Celebration, on a break from the Professional Bull Riders circuit.

Even though they could've invited the entire town, and everyone would've gladly attended, the bride and groom wanted to keep their special day intimate and elegant. They had limited the guest list to one hundred people. Actually, the vast amount of security dictated the cap.

Not long ago, Chelsea had been hounded by a particularly tenacious tabloid reporter whose antics had bordered on stalking. One of the objectives for the wedding was to make sure no rogue reporters got past the barriers. But that was security's task. They were trained professionals. So Lucy was banking on them doing their job so that Lauren could do hers.

That morning, Chelsea, Lucy and Juliette had prepared for the big day in Lucy's house, which was right next door to the barn. There was a brand-new bridal room inside the wedding barn, which Lucy had built during the renovation, but since Chelsea was family, they had opted to get ready at the house.

While Chelsea was having her hair, makeup and nails done, Lucy had been back and forth between the house and the barn, checking and double-checking that Lauren had everything in place.

"Everything will be fine," Lauren scolded when Lucy, in her long blue bridesmaid dress and black strappy sandals, her dark hair styled in an updo, had sneaked away from the bridal party for the umpteenth time to check on another detail. "I have my work order. All I have to do is follow it. Today, your job is to tend to Chelsea. You're not doing a very good job of that when you're over here checking up on me."

She was right. Lauren was good at this. She had common sense, good instincts and great people skills. It was why Lucy had hired her in the first place, and why she was trusting her to oversee this very important wedding. Plus, if something did go wrong, it wasn't as if Lauren wouldn't be able to find Lucy.

On the way back to the house, Lucy ran into Jude, who was looking tall and handsome, if not a little uncomfortable, in the traditional tuxedo Chelsea had picked out for Ethan's groomsmen—Jude and Zane—to wear during the wedding.

Jude had missed last night's rehearsal dinner because his schedule had forced him to take the redeye and arrive this morning, but he was here now, and that was all that mattered.

She hadn't had a chance to talk to him. So she grabbed the opportunity now.

"Hey, stranger." She gave him a big hug, sighing at how good it was for all three of the Campbell siblings to be together again. Lucy adored her brothers. Jude was the middle sibling; Ethan was the oldest. Jude was just as free-spirited and lonewolfish as Ethan was rooted and inclusive. Where Ethan had always been practical, Jude had marched to his own drum.

"We should have weddings more often if it will get you home," Lucy said, pulling back to take in his ruggedly handsome face. "Speaking of weddings, have you seen Juliette?"

Jude stiffened. "Not yet, but I hear she is part of the wedding party. So I'm bound to see her soon enough."

If the town of Celebration, Texas, had been taking wagers on which Campbell sibling would have been the first to marry, most people would have cast their vote for Jude. He and Juliette had been high-school sweethearts. Both of them had itchy feet and couldn't wait to see the world. Everyone thought they'd go off together. But they ran into trouble when Juliette won a scholarship to a college in England. The two of them had surprised everyone when they had broken up right before she went away to school. After she left, Jude had thrown his heart and soul into professional bull riding. It had been a bitter breakup. As far as Lucy knew, the two hadn't spoken since. Probably because about three months after the breakup, Jude had announced his engagement to a barrel racer he'd met at one of the competitions. The engagement hadn't lasted long, but the blow seemed to have killed any chance of reconciliation between him and Juliette. Still, weddings tended to cast magical spells over people. Lucy wasn't counting them out yet.

"Speaking of weddings," Jude said. "What's going on with you and Phillips?"

Lucy felt heat flame in the area of her décolletage and begin a slow creep up her face until it burned her cheeks, which she was sure were the color of the red rose pinned to her brother's lapel.

Just be cool.

"What do you mean?" she said, trying to be as nonchalant as possible.

Jude studied her for a moment before his gaze dropped to her belly. Instinctively, she crossed her hands in front of her. She wasn't showing yet, but she had a sinking feeling that her brother knew everything.

"I think you know what I mean," he said. "Ethan told me the good news. You should know that he can't keep a secret, and since I'm only here on a quick turnaround, I wanted to be sure I had a chance to say congratulations in private."

"Thanks," she said, her cheeks burning again. "But that really wasn't his news to tell. Is he broadcasting it to everyone?"

She hated to have to bring it up on Ethan's wedding day, but she needed to make sure the news didn't get out before she and Zane were ready. They still had a lot to figure out.

"Since I have to leave so soon and the wedding is going to be pretty all-consuming, I think he wanted to make sure I knew. Ethan might have a big mouth around family, but he can be pretty damn stoic around everyone else. He won't tell anyone else. I'm happy for you, sis. As long as you're happy."

For a moment she was afraid she would start weeping with relief and joy. That was precisely the reason she loved Jude so much. When she felt at odds with the rest of the world, he was always on her side. He never judged, and, in return, he expected the same nonjudgmental treatment. Actually, Jude did a good job of pretending like he didn't care what the rest of the world thought. But Lucy knew his cool act hid a tender heart.

"I am happy, Jude." She put her hand on her still flat belly. "I'm not gonna lie. This wasn't exactly planned, but it feels right. I'm home. I'm settled. This baby feels like a new infusion of life for the Campbell family."

She tried to ignore the twinge of conflict that twisted in her heart as she thought of Zane asking her to go with him to Ocala. She still hadn't decided what she was going to do. Why did everything have to be so difficult? Just when she thought everything was falling into place, everything... Well, at least she couldn't say everything *fell apart*. Because it hadn't. Leaving everything she'd worked so hard to build so that she could be with the only man she'd ever loved, who still couldn't say he loved her, too, was just *complicated*.

"It does feel like new life," Jude said. "I love the idea of being an uncle. Uncle Jude." He nodded his approval. "I like the sound of that. I'm going to be the cool uncle. Ethan will be the grouchy dude."

They laughed, because that pretty much summed up the situation. Although Ethan would never admit it.

"Does that mean you'll come home more often once the baby's born?"

"Every chance I get. I've got to run. I told Ethan I'd get him a Dr. Pepper. Apparently, Chelsea mandated that he not be outside roaming around and take the chance of them seeing each other before the ceremony. You know, all that bad-luck superstition. I didn't know they believed in that in England."

Lucy scrunched up her face. "Why wouldn't they believe that in England?"

Jude shrugged. "I'm a cowboy. Shows you what I know."

As he turned to leave, Lucy said, "Jude?"

He stopped and looked over his shoulder. "Yeah?"

"I've missed you."

He winked at her and pointed his finger in a quick gesture before he turned to complete his groomsmen mission.

She thought about asking him not to say anything to anyone else, but she knew he wouldn't. She knew Ethan wouldn't, either. It was important that both of her brothers knew and that both of them were happy for her. Ethan would probably be happier if she took the more traditional route and accepted Zane's proposal. But that was her decision and hers alone.

She stood there for a moment feeling safe and loved and secure… And more confused than she'd ever been in her entire life. Then she shook it off, because today wasn't about her. It was about Chelsea and Ethan. Two people who loved each other madly. Two people who wanted to be together, to spend the rest of their lives together because of *love*.

The barn had never looked more beautiful, with its string lights and candlelit lanterns. There were so many flowers that she couldn't turn her head without seeing blossom-pink and white peonies, scarlet-red roses and garlands of jasmine and ivy. All the flowers had been gathered from the Campbell ranch, and they perfumed the air. Lucy couldn't decide if it was like a scene from *The Secret Garden* or a page torn straight out of a story about a princess wedding.

Maybe both. Chelsea was almost a princess.

One thing was certain—love floated in the air from the hearts of all who were there to witness this joining of two lives. It mingled with the scent of all those flowers and the sound of the string quartet playing a slow, ethereal Celtic serenade. The beauty of the moment, its sheer, effortless perfection, made Lucy breathless and wistful.

She wanted *this*.

She was the first to walk down the aisle before maid-of-honor Juliette and then Chelsea. As Lucy made her way from the back of the room toward the dais, her gaze found Zane's and they held on to each other, an invisible thread of longing—or maybe it was *belonging*—binding them.

As Lucy took her place up front, Zane's gaze was still on her, even though Juliette was walking down the aisle. It brought to mind a saying—the best kiss is the one that has been exchanged a thousand times between the eyes before it reaches the lips. She didn't know who'd said it originally, but it was perfect. Almost as perfect as Pablo Neruda hearing the unsaid in a single kiss.

How could Zane look at her that way and not love her?

How would she ever know if he could love her if she didn't at least let him try?

Maybe if we got away from Celebration, we could figure out if we could be happy together.

After the officiant pronounced Ethan and Chelsea husband and wife, Lucy had never seen the pair of them look happier than they were in that moment. They had been through separate hells, but by the grace of all that was good, they had managed to find each other. It was Chelsea's first marriage and Ethan's second. Their path to each other hadn't been an easy road for either of them. They'd struggled, but they hadn't given up—or maybe they had, but once they'd found each other, they hadn't let fear and past failures keep them from what was good.

Lucy and Zane were the last of the bridal party to walk down the aisle during the recessional. He offered her his arm and it felt so natural to accept it. Just as natural as it felt to dance with him and be by his side all night long. Wasn't this how it always was between them?

She'd spent all these years wishing that Zane would fall in love with her, wondering why he was so blind. Maybe she was the one who'd been oblivious all these years.

At the end of the night, after everyone had eaten

and danced and celebrated Ethan and Chelsea, it was
time for the bride to throw her bouquet. A group of
eleven single women, including a reluctant Juliette,
who had done her best to avoid Jude during the moments when they weren't forced together as part of
the wedding party, gathered for the toss. Before she
turned around, Chelsea pinned Lucy with her gaze
and smiled. When she threw the bouquet of white
peonies, roses, jasmine and lilies over her shoulder,
it landed right in Lucy's hands.

Everyone cheered and chanted, "You're next!
You're next!"

Lucy wasn't sure if it was an omen. Maybe she
should've ducked out of the way.

"You did that on purpose," she said to Chelsea.
"Did my brother put you up to it?"

"No, I did," said Zane. "Will you please come
with me to Ocala to just see what you think?"

"You must be Zane's *fiancée*." Rhett Sullivan, the
owner of Hidden Rock Equestrian in Ocala, shook
Lucy's hand.

"Nice to meet you, Mr. Sullivan, I'm Lucy Campbell."

Lucy slanted a glance at Zane and he smiled at
her. There'd be hell to pay for fudging the fiancée
bit, he knew it. But maybe the power of suggestion
would help her make up her mind. At least he'd gotten her here.

"I'm pleased as punch that you could come out

and see the place with him. We think Zane will be a great addition to the Hidden Rock Equestrian family, but I know he's anxious to get your approval before he makes any decisions."

When Rhett turned his back to lead them toward the golf cart so that he could drive to the stables, Lucy shot Zane daggers.

"Your fiancée?" she said under her breath.

He shrugged. "I might have said something like that."

"Are y'all comfortable over at the house? That place is part of the compensation package. That's why we wanted y'all to get a chance to try it out tonight while you're here. My wife, Luann, just redecorated after the last GM and his family moved out. You just let her know if you need anything. Just holler and she'll see that you get it."

"Thank you, the place is lovely," Lucy said. "Please tell her I said so."

"Well, you'll get a chance to tell her yourself after the tour," Sullivan said as he climbed into the golf cart. "I'd planned on stealing our boy away to talk horse business. You and Lu can grab some lunch. It'll give you two gals a chance to get better acquainted. We're a tight-knit bunch around here and y'all will be spending plenty of time together while Zane and I are working."

Sullivan motioned for Lucy to sit in the golf cart's backseat and patted the seat next to him for Zane. He couldn't see Lucy's reaction because her hair fell in her face as she leaned forward to climb aboard the cart. Lucy was friendly and kind enough to not thumb her nose at Sullivan's hospitality, but he knew the guy dictating who Lucy would spend time with was probably a strike against his cause of making her fall in love with this place enough to move here.

Of course, it probably hadn't helped matters when she'd learned that he'd told Sullivan she was his fiancée. But it probably hadn't hurt. The reason he'd said it in the first place was because it was too complicated to try to explain their current situation to an older, more conservative Southern gentlemen like Rhett. And, yeah, Zane had been thinking positive at the time. At least Lucy was graciously playing along, but he was going to get it with both barrels once they were alone.

The Hidden Rock property was beautiful. Set in the verdant, rolling hills of Ocala, the farm went on forever and was surrounded by clusters of live oak trees dripping with Spanish moss. They'd even had to drive through a canopy of trees to get to the ranch.

Zane had heard a lot about Hidden Rock because its reputation spoke for itself. If he couldn't have his own farm, this place was everything he wanted. He could see himself getting up every morning and looking forward to going to work here.

"We built this place back in 1972," Sullivan said. "I know we went over the details when you visited before, but I'll give y'all the spiel again for your little lady's benefit."

Little lady? She was going to love that. Zane glanced over his shoulder at her.

"Did you hear that? All this is for you, dear."

She grimaced at him. Zane turned around before Sullivan could catch on. Then again, Rhett was a good ol' boy, who probably wouldn't even realize a *little lady* like Lucy would take issue with being called a little lady.

"Yeah, we're sitting on a little over eight hundred acres here. We have just about everything you could ever want when it comes to breeding and training Thoroughbreds. We've got a seven-eighths-mile dirt training track, a swimming pond for the horses. And if I remember right, at last count we had sixteen barns with four hundred and twenty-six stalls, one hundred and fifty paddocks and a hell of a lot of grazing fields. We've got hot walkers and round pens. You name it, we've got it. And if we don't have it, we can get it. But most importantly, we do everything with the horses' safety and development in mind. I don't mean to brag, but you're not going to find a better operation in north central Florida. Aw, heck, I'd even stick my neck out to say we are the best outfit in the entire southeast. We breed champions here, Zane. With your background, you'll fit right into our mission."

"Yes, sir," Zane said.

Sullivan drove around for a good half an hour talking about the various points of interest on the farm. Zane wondered if Lucy's eyes were glazing over, but then he realized he wasn't giving her enough credit. She'd grown up among the horse crowd in Celebration, but Hidden Rock was a completely different species from what they were used to. This place was magnificent. It was a chance to make a name for himself. A chance to carve out a future for his family.

As Rhett parked the cart in front of a gargantuan white antebellum house with columns like something from *Gone with the Wind*, their host turned around and placed a beefy arm along the seat back and trained his attention on Lucy.

"What did you think of that?" He didn't give her a chance to answer. "It's a real opportunity for this man of yours. Yeah, we got résumés from some people with more experience, but I go on attitude. Your boy here has great potential. This is what I'd call a win-win situation. That means we both have something to offer each other. A guy with talents like Zane's can do big things at a place like Hidden Rock. And Hidden Rock can certainly benefit from his talents. So, I'm counting on you to work your magic on him and tell him everything you love about this place. I sense that's what he's waiting for before he tells me he's joining the Hidden Rock family."

"Lucy, darling, it's lovely to finally meet you."

Luann Sullivan leaned in and air-kissed Lucy's

cheeks, Euro-style. The woman was nothing like what Lucy had imagined. Her husband had painted a picture of a demure woman whose sole purpose was servitude, the consummate *little lady* who lived to fetch and please.

Luann was tall, blonde and regal. The type of woman who seemed more at home in jodhpurs, riding boots and a diamond ring the size of a headlight than being at a guest's beck and call. One look at Luann Sullivan and Lucy understood that any *fetching* would be performed by the huge staff, some of whom served their luncheon by the pool on the terrace of the Sullivans' six-thousand-square-foot home.

How Luann and Rhett Sullivan fit together seemed a mystery. He was Budweiser and plaid button-down shirts; she was Veuve Clicquot and Cartier. No doubt, he was one of those Southern men who had so much money he didn't have to worry about looking like he had anything. So, it was probably the money and the horses that had brought them together.

Later, Lucy and her hostess enjoyed lobster salad and sparkling mineral water under the biggest and most silent outdoor ceiling fan Lucy had ever seen. It stirred up a gentle breeze, rendering the punishing Florida humidity powerless, as it provided a pleasant place for the women to enjoy the panoramic view of Hidden Rock.

Luann was a timeless beauty. Her ageless, effortless elegance was probably a by-product of good

genes, faithful sunscreen use, fresh air and sunshine.
And probably regular Botox.

"Are you a horse lover like your husband-to-be?"
Luann asked.

Lucy blanched at the reference to Zane and hoped
Luann didn't notice. "I was raised with horses. My
family has a small breeding farm in Celebration,
Texas. My brother is running the ranch now."

"Is that so?" Luann smiled and leaned in. "What's
the name of the ranch? Perhaps I've heard of it."

"It's called the Triple C. My family's name is
Campbell."

"*Ahh*, how nice."

Translation: *I've never heard of it.*

"Do you ride?" Luann asked. "If so, let's take the
horses out before you leave."

It had been a long time since Lucy had ridden a
horse, and even at her best, she'd never been much
of an equestrian. Not to mention, riding probably
wouldn't be the best thing for the baby. Her doctor
had told her she could participate in mild exercise
that her body was already used to, but now wasn't
the time to try anything new. Or go riding after all
these years.

But she couldn't share that with Luann.

"It's been a long time since I've ridden," Lucy
said. "I work a lot these days. It doesn't allow me a
lot of free time."

Luann smiled one of those gracious, practiced
smiles that made it seem like she was genuinely in-

terested in Lucy's workaholic ways, but Lucy suspected she was just being polite.

"What do you do, dear?"

"I run a wedding barn."

"A wedding barn? What is that?"

"It's a barn that has been spruced up to provide a
rustic venue for weddings."

Luann laughed. "Of course! You'll have to excuse
me. Rhett and I have been married for so long that
I'm not up on the latest in wedding trends. We have
a daughter who is in her twenties, but she's not the
least bit interested in settling down. Your job sounds
fascinating. Will you try to find similar work when
you move here?"

"Oh, well, I'm not sure about that. Actually, I own
the venue. It's an old barn on my family's property
that we renovated."

Luann waved her hand. "There are a number of
ramshackle barns around here that I'm sure you
could work your magic on. Are you into the DIY
craze? It's a great way to keep busy." Something in
the tilt of the woman's head and the polite tone of
her voice seemed dismissive.

"We were featured in *Southern Living* magazine
and named one of 'The Most Beautiful Wedding
Barns in the South.'"

As a general rule, Lucy hated to brag. She had
framed the magazine cover and the portion of the
article that featured the Campbell Wedding Barn.
But generally, she let the venue speak for itself. She'd

only mentioned it now because Luann Sullivan didn't seem to understand that it wasn't just any old barn. It was a tie to her family. It had history and sentimental value that she couldn't simply recreate in Ocala's plethora of *ramshackle barns*. But how did you explain that to someone who came from a completely different world and had an obvious vested interest in making her fall in love with Ocala so that Zane would take the job?

You didn't.

Instead, Lucy smiled and nodded, borrowing a page from her mama, who used to insist, if you can't say something nice, be quiet.

So she listened to Luann, who obviously had little interest in ramshackle barns. She had switched the subject to her glory days as an Olympic dressage champion and Ocala's horsey crowd. Curiously, though she called herself an Olympic *champion*, she didn't mention winning a medal. Lucy had to bite her tongue to keep from asking, but she managed to resist.

It went against every bone in her body to be so passive, but she was feeling prickly and impatient. If her discontent came through as attitude, it might make things difficult for Zane. No matter her own trepidations and irritations, she would never do that to him. This could be a very good opportunity for him. The boss man was obviously gaga over him, certain that Zane was the man for the job.

Lucy dug deep to try to pull herself out of the

funk. If she put her own wants and needs aside, she was truly happy for him. She wanted good things for Zane. She only wished those good things were located in Texas.

Later that evening, the Sullivans hosted a barbecue. It wasn't specifically in Zane's honor, but it bore a strong resemblance to a welcome party.

She hated to jump to snap conclusions, but this didn't seem like it was going to work for her. She hadn't even been in Florida for twelve hours and already she was homesick for Celebration. This coming from a girl who at one point in her life couldn't wait to get out and see the world. But all that time away had proved to her that home was where her heart lived. Try as she might, she couldn't muster the enthusiasm she would need to pack up everything and relocate with a man who was only in this relationship because she was carrying his child.

She wouldn't dream of asking him not to take the job. How could she? But by the same token, how could he ask her to give up everything she'd worked so hard to build?

All of that was driven home when a woman who bore a striking resemblance to Luann, only younger and sexier, walked in and turned every head in the room. Her outfit, a shimmery little white dress that accentuated her perfect long blond hair and showcased her perfectly tanned long sleek legs, probably cost more than Lucy's entire wardrobe.

Damn her.

Lucy watched as she picked Zane out of the crowd and floated over.

"Hey there, Zane Phillips," she said, flirting with her eyes. "I told Daddy you are the man for the job. I'm so glad he listened."

So, this was the daughter who had no interest in settling down. Lucy's heart sank. The woman was tall and perfect and model gorgeous. Now that Lucy saw her up close, she realized she bore a striking resemblance to Blake Lively, only prettier. If that was possible.

Funny, Zane hadn't mentioned *interviewing* with the daughter when he'd returned from his first trip to Florida. But she had taken enough of an interest to recommend him to *Daddy*.

Daddy had listened.

"Hi, Taylor," Zane said. "Taylor Sullivan, this is Lucy Campbell."

She noted that this time he didn't introduce her as his fiancée.

Taylor's cool gaze slid to Lucy, lighting on her as if she'd just noticed her standing there.

Taylor flashed a perfect smile. "Nice to meet you, Lucy Campbell."

She turned back to Zane. "When do you start?"

"I haven't accepted the position yet," Zane said.

"Yet." Taylor looked confident. "Let me know when you do."

Zane's chin was cocked. Lucy wondered if he was making an effort to not let his gaze drop to the bit of

Taylor's cleavage peeking out to greet him. It was tasteful, but it did beckon the eye. Taylor was exactly Zane's type. Lucy had been in this position too many times not to recognize it. She was definitely fluffy-woodland-pet material. Only, she seemed smarter and had a decent name. And she came from a family with so much money her *daddy* could buy both Ocala and Celebration with his pocket change.

Lucy had Googled Rhett Sullivan after a staff member had transported her by golf cart away from Luann and the big house to the beautiful three-bedroom ranch-style home that would be part of Zane's compensation package. She'd learned that Rhett was a fourth-generation Floridian whose family had made its money in the sugarcane industry. Rhett and Luann Sullivan were both on several lists of the nation's wealthiest individuals. It seemed Lu had brought quite a dowry to the marriage.

"See you," Taylor promised as she floated away.

Zane had a funny look on his face.

So it began. Well, that hadn't taken long.

"I see you already have a Florida fan club," Lucy said.

"I do? What do you mean?"

"Oh, come on," Lucy said. "Don't be coy. She digs you. And I'd say she's just your type."

"Seriously?"

Lucy nodded. "Seriously. But you know what? I am exhausted. I'm going to call it a night. But you feel free to stay and mingle with the natives."

It was burning her tongue to suggest that it would

be in bad taste to sleep with the boss's daughter before he'd formally accepted the job, but she swallowed the bitter words, because it would sound, well, *bitter* and snarky.

Even if it was good advice.

"If you're not staying, I'm not staying," Zane said. "Let's at least pay our respects to the Sullivans."

"Zane, you haven't even eaten yet. You need to stay. This party is essentially for you. Really, I'll be okay. I just have a headache. It's been a long day after the flight and the tour."

"You need to eat," he said.

She was just about to say that there was plenty of food in the well-stocked ranch house kitchen, but Rhett Sullivan appeared in front of them. After some cordial small talk, he said, "Little lady, I need to borrow your boy. Now, you mix and mingle and make some friends. These are going to be your people and they're all dying to meet you."

"I'll be right back," Zane said. Then he mouthed, *Don't go.*

It was the first time in her life she'd experienced the sensation of being simultaneously relieved and heartbroken.

Relieved to be able to make such an easy exit.

Heartbroken because she knew she would never fit in in Ocala.

Chapter Nine

Zane got back to the house about an hour and a half after he'd realized Lucy had left the party.

"I'm sorry," he said. "I would've been back sooner, but I had a hard time getting away from Rhett."

Sullivan had kept signaling the servers to refill their bourbon glasses and introducing him to people. Zane had quit sipping his drink, but short of being rude, he'd had little control over the introductions. Finally, when Rhett, who had been tossing back his drinks like shots and refreshing every time a server offered, was blotto and distracted by a sexy blonde who looked dangerously close to his daughter's age, Zane had slipped away.

Lucy shook her head. "Zane, you shouldn't have

left the party. Please don't cut the night short because of me. Go back." She shooed him away with the wave of her hand and turned her attention back to one of those celebrity magazines she loved so much. She was curled up on the couch with the magazine, reading and sipping a mug of something that smelled warm and minty. She'd changed into an oversize T-shirt, piled her dark hair on top of her head and scrubbed her face clean of makeup.

"You look like you're settled in for the night," he said.

She nodded but didn't look up from her magazine.

He sat down on a chair and started taking off his boots.

"What are you doing?" she asked. "It's only nine o'clock. I would imagine the party is just getting started. You can't just cut out."

"I can't? Really? I just did." He lined his boots up on the floor at the end of the expensive-looking coffee table. The place was so nice, he probably should've taken off his shoes outside or at least left them on the wood floor and not the white area rug that resembled a pelt of the world's largest sheepdog. He would've described it as shaggy, but something told him it probably cost a fortune.

He got up and moved his boots to the door, came back and sat down on the couch next to her.

"Zane, you need to go back." She nudged him with her bare foot.

"It's been a long day." He grabbed her foot and put it in his lap. "I'm peopled out."

What he really wanted to say was that he didn't want to go back without her. But that wouldn't be fair. He knew this wasn't fun for her. She'd been a good sport all day, playing the supportive, if not pretend, fiancée. It was late and he knew she was tired. Even at this stage, the baby sapped her energy.

"The master schmoozer is peopled out? The end of the world must be near."

She closed the magazine and tossed it onto the coffee table. There was a picture of one of those royal dudes on the cover. Henry or Hank or Harry or whatever his name was. Lucy would know. She knew them all. Even before meeting Chelsea she'd always been obsessed with royalty. She probably should've been born a princess—

He should treat her like one.

She stretched her legs and put the other foot in his lap, too. He started massaging both feet. She had nice feet. They were soft and her toenails were always painted some color. Tonight, they were a bright red.

"Did you talk to Taylor after I left?" She smiled and quirked a brow at him in a way that was so Lucy.

"No, I didn't talk to Taylor. Why, are you jealous?" he teased. "If you are, it means you care."

"I'm not jealous. I'm just realistic. She likes you. I can tell."

He moved his thumb in firm circles along the bottom of one foot. She seemed to melt into it.

"I noticed you didn't deny the fact that being jealous means you care," he retorted.

She shrugged, still not disputing it.

"Taylor was just being friendly," he said. "Hospitable."

"I'm sure she is. She could be *the one*, Zane. Don't write her off."

"You *are* jealous." He slid his hand along her silky leg as he moved from one foot to the other.

"Why would I be jealous? This is the story of our life. You're a serial monogamist. I've watched you in action for years. You've been on your own for a while now. It's about that time in your cycle when you settle down with another temporary distraction."

"We've both got our history, Lucy. Nothing we can do to change it. All that matters is where we go from here."

He reached out and tucked a strand of hair behind her ear that had fallen down from her bun. She tilted her head toward him until her cheek rested on his hand.

"They say the past is where you learn the lesson, the future is where you apply the lesson. I guess we've both experienced enough loss and lessons in our lives to make us how we are. Maybe it's too late for us to change. For me it's holding out for true love, for you it's not believing in it."

He stroked her cheek. "I guess we're polar opposites when it comes to that. It's kind of a miracle we've always gotten along so well."

"You know what they say, opposites attract. I guess that means you're the yin to my yang."

He laughed. "Whatever that means. If it's good, then yeah, I guess so."

"It's a very good thing."

She was quiet for a moment as they sat together on the couch. Somehow, over the course of the conversation, she'd scooted closer. Zane was determined to not fill the silence, to let her do the talking.

"When I lost my parents, I realized what it was like to have the bottom fall out of my world," Lucy said in a small voice. "But seeing how much my mom loved my dad just deepened my belief in the power of love. After their accident, when my dad died, my mom was never the same. She only lasted ten months after he left her. I've always believed she died of a broken heart."

Zane reached out and took Lucy's hand. He squeezed it and shut his eyes for a moment. "I remember how hard that was for you, Lucy. I am so sorry."

"I couldn't do anything to help her," she said. "Truth be told, I never thought she'd die. I was only fourteen. I thought she was invincible. You know, that she'd never *do that to me*. That she'd never leave me. Like it was all about me. But she did leave—she left Ethan, Jude and me. She loved our dad so much, she just lost her will to live and wasted away—" Her voice broke and he saw her throat work as she swallowed.

They were both silent for a moment.

"See, that's the thing about love," he said. "When you open yourself up like that, you risk getting hurt."

"But it can be so worth it. I wish you could see that."

He pulled her into his arms and held her, just held her, for a long time.

"You were too young to lose your mom," he whispered in her ear. "I'm so sorry for all the pain that caused you. But I'm not sorry for who you've become because of it. You are one of the strongest, most amazing people I have ever met in my entire life."

He moved his head so that his cheek was on hers. The next thing he knew, her mouth, soft, warm and inviting, had found his.

It vaguely registered that he shouldn't be doing this—again. She was vulnerable right now. But he was kissing her and she was kissing him back and the realization that they both knew what they were doing overrode the doubt.

The taste of her lips awakened his hunger more than it satisfied his craving for her. Need churned inside him, and for an endless moment he let himself be raw and vulnerable. Maybe loving her could fix everything that was broken inside him.

A moan, deep in his throat, escaped as desire coursed through him, a yearning only intensified by the feel of her lips on his, her body in his arms. His one lucid thought as Lucy melted into him was that she tasted familiar: smooth and sweet as home-made caramel and warm…like peppermint and fire.

It made him reel. He never wanted to breathe on his own again. He could be perfectly content right here with her in his arms for the rest of his life.

His hands slid down to her waist and held her firmly against him as his need for her grew and pulsed, taking on a life of its own.

He slowly released her, staying forehead to forehead as if he was drawn to her magnetically. He reached out and ran the pad of his thumb over her bottom lip.

"We said we weren't going to do this again," he whispered. "If we don't stop now…you know what'll happen."

"I know," she said. "I don't care. I want you."

He claimed one more kiss. It took every bit of strength in him, but he knew this was as far as they should go.

"What about the baby?" he said, his lips brushing hers.

"As long as we don't do anything acrobatic," she said, "my doctor said we should be fine. In fact, she told me it would be a good way to relax."

She'd thought about this happening again. That was all he needed to know.

The nearness of her, the heat they generated, sent electricity ripping through him. Then, when she gently nipped at his bottom lip, he warred with the need to take her right there on that ridiculous shaggy rug. He wanted to make love to her in a way that would reach back through the years and right all the wrongs and erase all the hurt both of them had experienced.

Zane didn't know if this was love, but this thing between them felt deeper and more right than anything he'd ever felt in his entire life. Lucy's essence had imprinted on his senses. For the first time, his heart was no longer his own.

Lucy got to her feet and took Zane's hand. She led him to the first bedroom she came to.

She wasn't going to allow herself to dwell on the difference between love and lust, on where they were going versus where they'd been. For once, she was fully in the moment. All that mattered was how she needed him and the way his hands felt on her. He made her feel powerful and strong and desirable. No one had ever made her feel like this before. She had never felt like this for anyone. It had always been Zane.

Slowly, they undressed each other, their clothes falling away until they stood naked in front of each other in the dim light. The bedroom was lit only by light from the lamp they'd left on in the living room. It filtered in through the open door.

For a brief moment, his tender gaze searched hers, as if he was giving her one last chance to turn away.

"We don't need to worry about birth control," he

said. "But I wanted you to know that I haven't been with anyone else since we were together."

She answered him with a kiss so deep that it had him walking her backward to the bed and gently lowering her onto it. He straddled her, keeping his weight on his knees as he traced gentle circles on her belly. It gave her a chance to see him, to drink in all his hard, masculine beauty. Their only other night together had been such a rush and a blur; she hadn't been able to live in the moment. Tonight was different.

She wanted to photograph him with her mind, commit him to memory. Just in case this was the last time— No!

There was no "just in case." There was only right now. And it was exactly what she wanted. She wanted him. She needed him. He traced a path from her belly to her breasts and smoothed his palm over the sensitive skin, making her inhale sharply.

"You are so beautiful," he said.

She felt beautiful. He made her feel beautiful.

He bent down and closed the distance between them, possessing her lips. She opened her mouth to let him all the way in. She ran her hands down his arms, then up his back, learning the planes and edges of his body. He was at once brand-new and hauntingly familiar. Now his lips were trailing a path over her collarbone, then dipping down into the valley between her breasts.

All the nights she'd dreamed of being with him

like this seemed real now. As if those dreams had come from an alternate reality, where the two of them had always been in love. A land of alpha and omega, or maybe it was a place where there was no beginning or end. Just a place where their souls had always lived, endlessly entwined.

He deftly shifted his body so that he was stretched out beside her. She turned to face him so that they lay stomach to stomach, bare chest to breasts. The feel of his skin against hers almost put her into sensory overload. She was so aware of him, of the two of them fused so closely, that it seemed they were joined body and soul. The entire world evaporated as they touched and caressed and explored each other, each taking turns bringing the other to the outer edges of ecstasy.

The feel of him worshipping her body with his mouth and hands brought out all the desire and longing that had been bottled up in her since the night they'd first made love.

She'd never felt this way about anyone. She wasn't sure what was going to happen after tonight, but she wasn't going to think about that now. All she cared about was the hot tender way he was touching her and how she wanted to live inside the bubble of this moment, suspended in time and space forever.

No Ocala. No Celebration. Just them. Together. Now.

Tonight they existed in the here and now. Just them. No one else. Tonight she intended to make love to him like there would never be another moment like this one. Because there might not be—

He preempted the wayward thought with kisses that found their way to her abdomen and circled her belly button. Then, gently pushing her onto her back, he took a detour and kissed the insides of her thighs. She inhaled sharply and her eyes widened.

"Why did we decide it was a good idea to just be friends?" His voice was soft and breathless in the darkness.

"I don't know. It was a dumb idea. We are too good together."

He flashed a wicked smile at her as he climbed back toward her. With a commanding move he turned her onto her side. He spooned her, kissing her neck and pulling her body snugly against him. She could feel the hard length of him pressing against her, and she gave in to the temptation to slide her body down and take him inside of her.

He found his way so naturally, entering her with a tender, unhurried push, that the sensation made her cry out. He gently inched forward, going so very slowly and being so careful. As her body adjusted to welcome him, she joined him in a slow rocking rhythm.

Another groan bubbled up in her throat as she savored the heat that coursed between them. It seeped into her bones as she reveled in the feel of him inside her. She drew in a jagged breath, determined to not rush things. Determined to savor every last delicious second.

"Zane," she whispered.

Her sighs were lost in his kiss. He touched her with such care and seemed to instinctively know what her body wanted.

Pleasure began to rise and she angled her hips up to intensify the sensation. Their union seemed so very right that she cried out from the sheer perfection of it.

"Let yourself go," he said, his voice hoarse and husky. "Just let go, Lucy."

Maybe it was the heat of his voice in her ear, more likely it was the way he made her body sing, but the next thing she knew, she had fallen over the edge in a free fall of ecstasy.

Again, he wrapped his arms around her, holding her tightly, protectively, until she had ridden out the wave.

She turned her head so she could see him, so she could breathe in the scent of him, of their joining, needing to get as close to him as possible. Still inside of her, he held her tight. She lost herself again in the shelter of his broad shoulders and the warmth of his strong arms.

"How was that?" His voice was a raspy whisper.

His eyes searched her face.

"It was great. I can hardly speak."

He smiled. "And we're not finished yet."

Zane buried his head in the curve of her neck

and started the rhythmic motion again, slow, at first, building to a delicious pace. Again, she felt the energy building inside her body, like a starburst glowing warm, hot, hotter—until they both arrived at the brink together. It didn't take long before their bond, coupled with the pulsing of their bodies, carried them over the edge together. They were both sweaty and spent, and he cradled her against him. They lay together for a long time, their bodies so close, it was hard to tell where she stopped and Zane began.

Later, when Lucy turned onto her other side to face him, Zane stared into her deep brown eyes and felt the mantle of his life shift. All of a sudden, without explanation, *everything* was different.

How could that happen now when it had never happened to him before? He hadn't thought he was capable of experiencing it, because he'd never had a feeling like this.

He was in love with Lucy's laugh, in love with her mind, in love with the way she was able to keep him in line without making him feel as if she was trying to change him. He was in love with the way she felt in his arms right now, the smell of her skin and the way she gazed up at him with a certain look in her eyes that was equal parts sassy confidence and vulnerability. In her eyes, he glimpsed everything he already knew about her and all the things he had yet to discover.

In a staggering instant, he had the overwhelming

need for her to be the first face he saw in the morning and the last face he saw before he closed his eyes and drifted off to sleep at night. He wanted to be the shelter where she sought refuge and the storm who swept her off her feet.

The question was, did he have it in him? Could he be that for her on any ordinary Tuesday night, when they were both tired and life wasn't romantic or even fun anymore?

She deserved someone who was crazy about her all the time, someone who adored her and loved her the way she'd always dreamed of being loved. He wanted to prove to her that he was a good man. But that added up to ripping open his heart and rendering it vulnerable, leaving it in her hands.

This was *Lucy.* If he could trust anyone, it was Lucy. Still, the magnitude of it—of this rush of feelings, the slow, gradual coming back down to earth—scared him to death. But it was too late now. He'd already passed the point of no return.

Now he needed to figure out what to do.

"Zane?" Lucy's eyes searched his face. "Are you… okay?"

"I am better than okay," he finally said.

He kissed her deeply, pulling her to him so tightly that every inch of their bodies merged. He hadn't particularly cared how close he'd felt to other women after they'd been intimate. But this was different. He needed the connection. Not just body to body, but eye to eye and soul to soul.

As they'd made love, three words had been building in his heart. Now they'd worked their way to the tip of his tongue.

He turned onto his back and threw an arm over his eyes, trying to catch his breath. *Come on, man... You're caught up in the moment. Don't say things you don't mean.*

The problem was, he *wanted* to mean it. With all of his heart and soul.

Even so, meaning "I love you" and living it the way Lucy expected were two very different orders.

He couldn't bring himself to say the words out loud.

The next morning, they didn't have time for things to get weird. Zane had an early breakfast with Rhett Sullivan. He was gone by the time Lucy woke up.

She was relieved, really.

Okay, so she would've liked to have had a chance to read the relationship barometer before he'd dashed out the door, but this time alone gave her a chance to do a little soul searching of her own. Time to sort out why the best night of her life left her with such a feeling of dread.

There had been no breakfast invitation from the Sullivans for Lucy. She hadn't wanted or expected one, but it did seem glaringly indicative of what she should expect if she was to move to Ocala with Zane. Despite Rhett Sullivan's insistence that the Hidden Rock crew was *family*, Lucy could already tell it wouldn't be an easy task for her to infiltrate the ranks. She just wasn't cut from that cloth. Maybe in time she and Luann would grow to be friendly—friendly-ish—but Lucy knew the truth. It would never happen.

Luann Sullivan was a wonderful woman, Lucy was sure, but the two of them had zero in common. Not only that, but Ocala was also a different world from everything Lucy wanted from life. Just like Luann, it was lovely. There wasn't a thing wrong with either Luann or this place. But neither of them was for her.

Zane, though… Hidden Rock was the perfect place for him.

Hence Lucy's dark cloud of sadness. She tried with all her heart to be happy for him. She would never stand in his way, but the only thing she'd managed to accomplish by accompanying him on this trip was to know beyond a shadow of a doubt that she could not move there with him.

Zane must've had an idea of what was coming, because the two of them didn't discuss the possibility of her moving to Ocala until after their plane had landed at Dallas/Fort Worth International Airport and the car that Sullivan had hired to pick them up had delivered them to Lucy's house.

"Okay," Zane said after he'd put his suitcase in his truck. "I've given you time to mull it over without bugging you about it. But I have to know. What do you think? It's a pretty great place, isn't it?"

Zane had managed to slip out of Rhett Sullivan's grasp without giving him a solid answer. Sullivan had granted him twenty-four hours to mull over the employment package and give him an answer. The boss had even complimented his negotiation skills. Sullivan said while he'd have preferred to solidify the offer before Zane left, his needing to think it over was a feather in Zane's cap, but a guy like Sullivan had to have been pretty confident that he would get what he wanted in the end. Men like that always did.

"I'm glad I got to see Hidden Rock, because now I know without a doubt it is the perfect job for you."

It really was. The salary was twice the amount he was making at Bridgemont. And that didn't even count the house and the truck allowance. Plus, it went without saying, all the bourbon he could drink.

She braced herself for what she knew was coming next.

"Can you see us raising our child there?" Zane asked.

She wanted to tell him exactly how she felt, but she couldn't form the words.

She loved her life in Celebration. She loved her friends and family. She loved her wedding barn. Even though she'd jumped from one thing to another in the past, it was clear that every mistake and wrong turn she'd made had prepared her for the life she was living in Celebration. She was established here. Even though both of her parents were gone, her family was here. And she had friends, lots of friends, in Celebration. If she moved to Ocala, she would have Zane, but she wouldn't really *have* him.

As good as she and Zane were together, he still wasn't sure how he felt about her. Or at least he couldn't tell her how he felt. That was an answer in itself. She'd known Zane long enough to understand that he was moody, that he could blow hot and cold.

If she moved to Ocala, they would be pretending to be a family, and all the while Lucy would live in fear that the spell would wear off and he would grow discontent. If that happened, like Cinderella at the stroke of midnight, her coach would turn into a pumpkin and her dress would revert back to rags. All too soon, her Prince Charming would start feeling trapped, the same way his own daddy had felt.

That spelled disaster.

The only way she and Zane could make this coparenting arrangement work was if she didn't hold on to him too tightly. And that was why she had to let him go.

As she tried to gather her thoughts, she busied herself cleaning nonexistent dust off the potted philodendron on her windowsill.

"Did I ever tell you about the recurring dream that I used to have?" she said.

He hesitated. She didn't have to turn around to know that he was scowling because he thought she'd changed the subject. And she hadn't. He'd see.

"No."

"Well, once upon a time, I had this crazy recurring dream." Her back was still to him because she couldn't look at him. It was all she could do not to cry. "I dreamed that one day you would look at me and suddenly realize you loved me and couldn't live without me. In that dream, you'd suddenly see me and say, 'It's you, Lucy. It's always been you.'"

He was silent for a long moment.

Finally, he said, "And then what happened?"

"We got married and lived happily ever after, of course. Though, it's only fair that you know there were no fluffy woodland pets in this fairy tale."

"I would've been surprised if there were."

She swiped at her tears and picked up the watering canister to give the plant some water and herself something else to focus on. She didn't know what she would do next—she was running out of busy-work. Pretty soon, she would have to turn around and face him. She didn't want to, because once she did, the clock would strike midnight and everything would be over.

"You're not moving to Ocala with me, are you?"

She shook her head.

"I probably shouldn't even have visited," she said. "I have to be honest, I knew before we arrived that I couldn't move there."

"It really isn't what you want, is it?"

She shook her head again and set down the can.

"What about last night?" he asked.

"Last night was one of the most beautiful nights of my life—" She choked on her words. "But it doesn't change the fact that if I moved to Ocala with you, we would live together in a weird state of limbo that's not platonic, at least not for me, but definitely not love, at least not for you. Zane, I would give birth in a strange city, without a support system beyond you. You're a whole lot of good man, but you're going to be busy with your new job, which involves a fair amount of schmoozing at events like that barbecue. I'm truly happy that you've found your place. That's why you must take that job. But I can't go with you."

Thinking about how good this was for him helped her get ahold of herself. She turned to face him. He looked as miserable as she felt.

"What am I supposed to tell the Sullivans when they ask about you?" Zane said. "About why you're not moving with me?"

"Tell them the truth. That we were never really engaged. I'm sure Taylor will be thrilled to know you're not otherwise encumbered."

He winced.

"Zane, I'm not being snarky. I only want what's best for you. And for our child. Think about it— moving to Florida, where everything is fresh and shiny and brand-new, maybe you'll meet someone and realize you don't want it to be just a temporary fling. Maybe your soul mate is somewhere in Ocala and you'll finally know what it feels like to fall in love."

"Would you stop with the *love* talk already?" he said. "Love has nothing to do with this."

"Exactly. I know it doesn't, but it should. It should be all about love. And that's why we are where we are right now. Your we-don't-need-to-be-in-love theory will only work until you meet someone else and fall in love. Because just when you least expect it, the right woman is going to come along. You'll take one look at her and she will knock you off your feet. If you're tied to me, things will get messy. That's not a good way to coparent."

Zane didn't say anything. His walls were up. She wondered if he'd even heard her.

Lucy smiled through her hurt. She needed to find some way to salvage this. She didn't want him to go away mad.

"I have something for you," she said. "Stay here. I'll be right back."

A minute later, she returned with Dorothy's sketchbook. She handed it to him.

"What's this?"

"It was your mom's."

His brows knit together. "I know it was hers. Why do you have it?"

"Because I pulled it out of the garbage that night I came over with the movies."

Zane thumbed through it. "I don't remember throwing it away. Why would I throw this away? This was important. It's *her*."

"I wondered the same thing," Lucy said. "I think you had so much on you and you were so racked with grief that night, you didn't realize what you were doing."

The minute the words escaped her lips, she wished she hadn't said them, because that was the night they had made love, the night they had conceived a baby.

But it was true. That night Zane hadn't been in his right mind. She had seduced him in a vulnerable moment and… Well, the rest was history. As much as she had always dreamed of finding her happily-ever-after with him, she knew she wasn't going to find it like this. That was why, from this moment on, she needed to stop pretending like anything was going to change between them. She wasn't Cinderella. Zane was a good guy, but he wasn't a prince who was going to show up at her door with a glass slipper and suddenly declare his love.

"I hope you will take this with you as a reminder of what can happen if you don't follow your dreams." Zane did a double take, as if he was just realizing the parallels between his and Dorothy's situations. "Dorothy missed the *Guys and Dolls* ship. Her dream was in sight, but the ship sailed without her. Don't you miss out on your big opportunity. You'll still be a great father if you live in Ocala. Between the two of us, we will make sure you have a strong presence in our baby's life."

He didn't say anything. He was just staring at the sketchbook in his hands. Even though her heart was breaking, she was happy she'd saved it for him.

"You've already found your perfect job," she said.

"Maybe Ocala is the complete package. Taylor might not be a temporary fling. She likes you, Zane. Maybe someday all of Hidden Rock will be yours."

He glowered at her. "That's insulting. You're making me sound like a gold digger. Or like I'm not capable of making my own way."

He wasn't just surly. He was furious. But she was certain most of it stemmed from hurt pride.

"You're so smart and so very capable. If I made it sound like I thought otherwise, I'm sorry. If you weren't capable, a man like Rhett Sullivan wouldn't be willing to trust you with his empire. Now, you need to do the smart thing and take that job. Don't miss the boat."

Chapter Ten

Zane had been gone for a week, but it felt like a lifetime. Even though Lucy was swamped, consumed with prep for the Picnic in the Park celebration on the Fourth of July, it was all she could do to keep her mind on her to-do list.

Blake Shelton's song "Go Ahead and Break My Heart" came up on her Zane playlist. She'd compiled a bunch of songs that either reminded her of Zane or the lyrics pertained to their situation. She'd grouped them together on a playlist, which she streamed through the music app on her phone. Depending on her mood, she could either feel self-righteous, singing along to songs such as Nancy Sinatra's "These

Boots Are Made for Walkin'," or wallow in her own self-pity to tunes like "Desperado" by the Eagles.

Her favorite songs were a variety of singers and standards, with some fun '60s and '80s era music added for spice, but Zane loved country music and she'd added some country tunes that tugged at her heartstrings.

"Go Ahead and Break My Heart" was making her want to wallow, so she shuffled the mix and advanced to the next song. A Brett Eldredge song about going away for a while came up next. At least it was upbeat and not as sentimental as some on the list. She let it play.

When she got home tonight, maybe she should separate the songs into sub-playlists—self-righteous, empowering songs, and songs to wallow in self-pity and feel sorry for herself.

At least she wouldn't get emotional whiplash each time a new tune played.

She was just settling down and reviewing proposals for her business's website redesign when her phone rang.

"Campbell Wedding Barn, Lucy speaking."

"Is this Lucy Campbell?" a man asked.

"Yes, this is she. How may I help you?"

She really should consider hiring someone part-time to help with odds and ends and answering the phone. Every time it rang and she answered, she was pulled out of what she was doing and usually ended up going down some kind of rabbit hole that kept her from getting her work done. That was why her to-do list was so long.

"This is Nathaniel Phillips. I am Zane Phillips's dad. I'm hoping you can help me track down my son."

Lucy set down her pen. Oh, boy, she did not want to get in the middle of this. Zane had told her that his father had shown up at Dorothy's house the night he was moving out the last of her belongings. That was after Nathaniel had made an unwelcome appearance at Dorothy's funeral.

Now he was calling and asking her to put him in touch with Zane?

No way.

"Hi, Mr. Phillips. I'd be happy to take your number and pass it along to Zane the next time I talk to him."

The truth was, she and Zane hadn't spoken since he'd left for Ocala. She kept telling herself it was better that way. Clean break. That was why she hated the way her heart leaped at the thought of having an excuse to call him—even if it was to relay the news that his father was looking for him.

"I have something for him," Nathaniel said. "Are you sure you can't give me any information on how I can get in touch with him myself?"

Lucy swiveled in her desk chair so that she was facing the door that looked out into the cavernous belly of the barn. It was not as if the man was standing there in person. So she didn't need to run. But for some reason it made her feel better to focus on the way out.

"As I said, I'm happy to pass along your number to him. Would you like to give it to me?"

Reluctantly, Nathaniel rattled off some numbers. Lucy repeated them back to him.

"I'll make sure he gets the message," she said.

"Will you also tell him that I have something I know he wants. I'd like to give it to him."

"Absolutely. I'll let him know."

She hung up the phone. Nathaniel had something for Zane? What in the world could it be?

Before she could talk herself out of it, she retrieved her cell phone from her purse and dialed Zane's number. She knew it by heart. When it started ringing, her heart thudded like a staccato drumbeat.

This was crazy. They meant too much to each other to be in a standoff like this. Well, thanks to Nathaniel Phillips, she had a legitimate reason to break the ice. That was ironic.

But soon her optimism slipped a notch when she got Zane's voice mail. He used to always pick up when she called. In fact, she couldn't remember him ever not taking her call. In the span of time it took for his greeting to play out, she talked herself out of hanging up and decided to leave a message.

After all, she had promised his father she would let him know. She always tried to keep her promises. Plus, if she left a message, the ball would be in his court to call her back.

At the beep, she said, "Hey, you! It's me." That was how they used to greet each other on the phone when they called each other—back in the days when they called each other… When they were talking. She made an effort to infuse as much sunshine and sweetness in her voice as she could muster. "I hope everything is going well and that you're all settled in and liking your job. We miss you around here. Mrs. Radley is looking for a new benefactor for her tuna-noodle surprise." Okay, she needed to get to the point. It wasn't as if the longer she talked, the more likely it would be that he would pick up. That was not how cell-phone voice messages worked. "Also, I needed to let you know that your dad called me today asking for your phone number. Don't kill the messenger. I didn't give him your number. I asked for his and told him I would pass it along. So here it is."

She read the number twice. The second time, she said it slowly.

"Oh, and he asked me to tell you that he has something for you that he is certain you will want. So please call him. That's part of his message, not me being bossy. Just so you know. And you might give me a call if you can spare a few moments. That is me being bossy. I miss you."

She hung up before she could say anything else. She wished she could go back and erase that last part where she asked him to call her.

Ugh. That was embarrassing.

Oh, well. It was what it was. Now the ball was definitely in his court.

Peter Gabriel's "In Your Eyes" came up in the

shuffle. Lucy sighed and turned off the music because it wasn't helping matters. It was only making her sad. Even though some of the music was designed to let her wallow, the overriding effect wasn't supposed to be this.

She sat in silence for a few minutes, which was hardly better, but at least she didn't have to listen to Peter Gabriel going on about days passing and emptiness filling his heart.

There was wallowing and there was morose.

She'd made her choice to not move to Ocala with Zane. She needed to live with it.

Lucy had just wrangled herself back into work mode when there was a knock at the barn door.

"Oh, for God's sake. I am never going to get any work done."

She clicked over to her to-do list and typed in "hire part-time assistant."

The knock sounded again, and this time was more persistent. For a split second she worried that it might be Nathaniel Phillips. Then her heart went in a completely different direction—what if the reason Zane hadn't taken her call was because he was driving on his way back to see her?

She knew it was just wishful thinking, but it didn't stop the disappointment when she opened the door and saw Carol Vedder standing there with a handsome blond guy in tow.

"There you are, Lucy," Carol said. "We were just

about to leave. But I saw your car over there, so I knew you had to be around here somewhere."

Lucy had to blink away the stunning disappointment. First because it wasn't Zane at the door and second because she'd actually let herself hope that it was. She had gone from ridiculous to pathetic in less than sixty seconds. She needed to get ahold of herself.

"I am so sorry to keep you waiting," she said. "I was in the middle of something. I didn't realize you were coming by. Did I miss your call?"

She knew Carol hadn't called, and she should've been ashamed of herself for the little dig, but…

"No, I didn't call. I just picked up my nephew, Luke, from the airport. He lives in Houston, but he was flying in from a veterinarian conference in Los Angeles. Lucy, this is Luke Anderson. Luke, this is Lucy Campbell. The young woman I told you about."

"Nice to meet you, Lucy." He shook her hand. "Forgive us for barging in like this."

Lucy picked up on the note of embarrassment in Luke's apology and glimpsed the accompanying look in his eyes. He was humoring his aunt and was much too polite to roll his eyes the way Lucy sensed he wanted to.

"That is absolutely not a problem, Luke. It's nice to meet you. Would you like to come in?"

"If you're in the middle of something, I don't want to disturb you—"

"We will only be a minute," Carol said. "I brought

Luke by to help me carry a heavy box. For the Fourth of July picnic."

Lucy exchanged another commiserating look with Luke. He must've known that Carol's *moments* could last three weeks. That was when she realized Luke was *seriously* cute—like Ryan-Gosling-eat-your-heart-out cute. And he was a veterinarian. That meant he was good with animals.

And he wasn't Zane.

The father of her baby. The love of her life, who didn't return her feelings. The guy who was gone.

If she wasn't pregnant, she might've tried to be interested in this guy. He was from Houston. Far enough away that she could've had her space, but close enough to see occasionally—unlike the prohibitive fifteen-hour drive to Ocala.

But he wasn't Zane.

"Where is the box, Aunt Carol?" Luke asked.

"It's in the trunk, dear." She handed him her keys.

Both women watched him walk to the car. "He's a good catch, this one." Carol gestured in Luke's direction with her thumb.

He came back carrying a large package of paper towels. "This was the only thing that was in the trunk, besides my luggage."

Carol smiled. "Yes, that's it."

Something heavy, huh? Lucy was tempted to ask if she should get the hand truck, but that wouldn't be very nice. She knew Carol well enough to know she was immune to embarrassment. It would only make this awkward situation more awkward.

"I can take that," Lucy said.

"No, let Luke carry that for you. How about if he sets it in the kitchen?"

Lucy shrugged and motioned for them to come inside. As they walked toward the kitchen, Carol said, "Luke is going to be here for Picnic in the Park. He is also going to help me with a few handyman tasks around the house, because he's very handy. But I won't keep him too busy. He will have plenty of free time. Lucy, maybe you could show him around?"

Her mind raced. On one hand being nice to someone and showing him around wouldn't even necessarily have to be a date. But who was she kidding? It was obvious that Carol was trying to fix them up. What was she supposed to say? Sooner or later the entire town would know that she was expecting. It was her new reality and she had already accepted it. She'd also come to terms with the very real possibility that she probably wouldn't be dating for at least the next eighteen years or so.

That was fine. Her baby was all she needed.

What was the use of dating if her heart belonged to her child…and the baby's father?

Zane had picked up Lucy's message, but several days had gone by and he couldn't bring himself to call her back.

Not yet. The hurt was still too fresh. He got it. He totally understood Lucy's point of view and he wasn't going to be selfish. But that didn't mean he had to like the way things had turned out.

As far as his dad was concerned, there wasn't a chance in hell that he was calling him. He didn't want whatever scrapbook or memento the guy had dug up for him. He didn't need or want anything the jerk had to offer now—now that he and Ian were self-sufficient adults who needed nothing from others.

Nathaniel Phillips obviously thought that he was perfectly entitled to skip the messy parts of child rearing and jump into the hands-off easy part. Zane was having none of that.

He was too busy with his new job. He still hadn't adjusted to Ocala, to being there alone when he thought Lucy would be by his side. That was such a bastard way to think, that she should give up everything she'd worked for to follow him. One of the things he'd always loved most about her was her strength. She deserved only the best and she deserved the love she was so certain existed.

Hidden Rock was a great job, but it still didn't feel like his world. He knew he should give a new position a good six months— Hell, with an outfit like this, he'd be better off giving it more like a year.

He was drinking too much and working too hard, too many long hours. One night, when he'd gotten particularly shit-faced, he'd gone out with a bunch of the ranch hands and woken up the next morning with Lucy's name tattooed on his biceps. He'd never gotten a tattoo before. He didn't remember much about that night, but he did recall with dubious clarity telling the guy that Lucy was the love of his life. Uh… In his drunken stupor, he had used the *L* word. He had to laugh—even though it wasn't funny—because he could hear Lucy saying bourbon was his truth serum. The only other memory of that night that was vaguely clear was of the guy telling him if things didn't work out with her, he could always have the tattoo changed from *Lucy* to *Lucky*.

He was still contemplating whether he wanted to have it removed, though he'd heard that hurt like a son of a bitch. Because it would be more appropriate to have the word *UnLucky* tattooed on his arm to remind him of all he'd lost.

He was trying, but even though, in theory, Hidden Rock was supposed to be his dream job, he didn't love it here like he thought he would.

If he'd had this opportunity five years ago, things might have been different, but it didn't feel like it fit him now. This routine of getting up at dawn, working until sunset, drinking himself to sleep and then getting up and doing it all over again wasn't the stuff dreams were made of. Even though he was well aware of the theory that new jobs took a good half a year to break in, it didn't feel like the life he wanted to grow into. Not when another little life that had his blood—and hopefully Lucy's good looks, brains and charming personality—would be growing and changing every day in Texas without him. His dream job pinched. It just wasn't the same without Lucy. Instead of feeling fulfilled, he felt empty. And at the rate he was numbing himself, he'd end up working himself into an early grave. Of course, that was the only part of this equation that was under his control. He could stop drinking if he wanted to. Especially since his being healthy was key to him keeping his promise to be a good father to their child.

That was why when the boys asked him if he was going to join them at the bar after work on Thursday, he declined. It would do his liver some good to sit this one out. When he got back to the house, there was a man waiting for him on his front porch.

"Can I help you?" Zane asked. "This is a private residence. If you have business with Hidden Rock, the offices are about a mile up the way near the stables."

The guy had an envelope in his hand. "Are you Zane Phillips?"

Zane looked around warily. "I am."

"I have a certified letter for you. Please sign here."

What the hell—

Zane didn't owe anybody anything. He wasn't in trouble. Lucy wouldn't be sending him anything certified, would she? This wasn't about him not returning her call, was it? Her message hadn't sounded all that serious. If she needed anything, he definitely would've called her back.

"What's this about?" Zane asked.

"I have no idea. I'm just the messenger."

Since he had no reason to fear the envelope's contents and curiosity was getting the best of him, he signed, and the guy handed him the letter.

Zane took off his boots and left them on the porch, then let himself into the house.

The return address indicated the letter was from a Dallas-based law office. Zane picked up a letter opener on the kitchen cabinet and opened it.

The letterhead said the correspondence was from the law firm of Dorsey and Rogers. The content said that they had been retained by Nathaniel Phillips, who had been trying to locate him to bestow a gift upon him.

"A gift?" Zane said out loud.

His first inclination was to crumple up the letter without even reading it, but it dawned on him that if his father had gone to the trouble to hire an attorney to track him down so that he could give him a gift, maybe if he simply accepted whatever token he was trying to give him to appease his guilt, Nathaniel would go away and leave him alone. This might be the only reason that having fifteen hundred miles between him and Texas was a good thing.

But the next paragraph in the letter had Zane pulling out a kitchen chair and sitting down at the table to reread the letter to make sure he was understanding it right. Was his father actually trying to give him and Ian the property on Old Wickham Road?

That was what the letter said, even after Zane read

it five times to be sure. All he had to do was call the law firm to discuss the details.

The Fourth of July had always been one of Lucy's favorite holidays. Who didn't love an excuse to eat grilled hot dogs and potato salad and corn on the cob? And just when you thought you couldn't stuff another bite in your face, someone brought out the hot apple pie and homemade ice cream. Oh! And the fireworks. She had always adored the fireworks. Celebration's Fourth of July Picnic in the Park always culminated in a pyrotechnics display to rival Walt Disney World.

This year, however, she was hot and cranky. The smell of hot dogs made her want to toss her apple pie and she hadn't even had a bite of apple pie because it seemed even more unappealing than the hot dogs. She'd had to get downright testy with Pat Whittington, who had refused, on principle, to sign up early for the hot-dog eating contest.

"That's not how we do it," he insisted when he showed up and there wasn't a place for him at the competition table.

"Next year, Pat, why don't you chair the event and you can make the rules."

When he told her that she didn't have to be rude about it, she realized it really didn't matter whether anyone had preregistered or not. She didn't care.

That was when Juliette stepped in and they agreed to squeeze in Pat at the end of the table. Of course, he complained that he didn't have enough elbow room and that was why he lost last year… That was when Lucy walked away.

She bought herself a bottle of ice-cold water and took a seat on the rim of the huge fountain in the middle of the park and watched all of the flurry going on around her. The world wouldn't end if they squeezed one more person into the hot-dog eating contest. Though, for a fleeting second, she may or may not have wished that Pat Whittington choked on a wiener.

Then she chastised herself because that was not very nice.

"Nope, I wish him nothing but the best. May he get exactly what he deserves this year." She laughed to herself.

"Are you talking to me?" Luke Anderson was standing next to her smiling and looking just as handsome as he had the other day, when he and Carol had dropped by. Great, he'd caught her talking to herself. At this rate, maybe she should go home and crawl back in bed before she really embarrassed herself.

He was a good guy. He had obviously picked up on her trepidations as Carol had tried hard to push the two of them together, because she hadn't called or made any effort to "show him around," as Carol had put it. Then again, maybe he didn't find her as charming and alluring as Aunt Carol had thought he would.

Just as well.

"I wasn't," Lucy said. "But now that you mention it, I wish you nothing but the best, Luke."

He sat down next to her on the fountain. "Are you okay?"

She must've looked pretty stressed if he'd picked up on it.

She waved away his concern. "I'm fine. Just hot and thirsty. Just taking a break from all the fun."

"It's a great event. Do you organize it every year? I know Aunt Carol has been involved for a while."

"No, it's my first year on the committee."

And probably her last... Though she wasn't going to say that now. She likened organizing events to having accepted the challenge to eat an entire jar of peanut butter. At this point she was about three tablespoons away from finishing the whole jar. While she loved peanut butter, right now she never wanted to see it again.

She was too close to the situation and she was exhausted. And Zane wasn't here.

She fought the most ridiculous urge to cry. All she needed to do to prove to Luke that she was, indeed, crazy was to burst into tears right here in the middle of Central Park.

Thank goodness Lauren Walters chose that moment to walk over and say hello.

"Lucy, you have outdone yourself," she said. "It's the best Picnic in the Park ever. Everyone loves the food trucks. And the band you hired is fabulous. I'll help you next year if you'll stay on the committee. Oh, who's this?"

Lauren was eyeing Luke, who was still sitting next to Lucy on the edge of the fountain but was eyeing Lauren with a look that you didn't have to be a mind reader to know he liked what he saw.

Of course! They would be perfect for each other.

"Lauren, this is Luke Anderson. Luke is Carol Vedder's nephew. He's visiting from Houston. Luke, this is Lauren Walters. She's a good friend and she helps me out at the Campbell Wedding Barn occasionally."

"You're from Houston?" Lauren said. "I have family in Houston. I'm from there originally."

They started chatting, figuring out people they knew in common. "Lauren, if you have a few moments, would you show Luke around? Have you seen the food trucks, Luke?"

He hadn't. Lucy all but mentally brushed her hands together as she watched them walk away. She stood up feeling better than she had felt all day. Her work here was done.

She sighed. "I love a good romance. Especially when it's shiny and new."

Maybe her new role would be that she would be the fairy godmother—or the matchmaker. Either one would do.

With a renewed sense of spirit, Lucy made her rounds, ensuring that everything was running smoothly. It was good to stay busy. It gave her a purpose and blunted the empty feeling of being on the outside looking in as she watched families spending the day together, and lovers strolling hand in hand or feeding each other French fries from a food truck as they lounged on plaid picnic blankets spread over the park's green lawn.

Finally, as it was getting dark, Lucy prepared herself to make the address that the Picnic in the Park chairperson always delivered. She slipped into the bathroom at Café St. Germaine to freshen up. She splashed water on her face to cool off and reapplied her makeup, adding a little more than she had worn earlier because she felt like making an effort. She was proud of the work she had done. Proud of what she had accomplished with the event. She had raised money for the community, and, yes, she had even generated some good public relations for the Campbell Wedding Barn. Because there was hardly a better showcase of her event-planning skills than this important, sometimes unruly, community event. As she brushed her hair and secured it into a low ponytail, she realized it was also her debut as the new person she would become once she shared the news that she was expecting a baby.

She squared her shoulders and looked at herself in the mirror. Sure, she would've preferred the more traditional route—what she wouldn't have given for Zane to have been able to love her. But he was happy and that was everything.

She had a thriving business, a loving family, good

standing in a community that she loved. She had so many more blessings than some people. She put her hand on her stomach. Now was the time—a new phase—when she would start thinking less of herself and more of others.

A twinge of regret—of missing Zane, of loving Zane—was still there, but she would live with it. The two of them were happy in their separate lives. That would go a long way toward creating a happy life for their child. She realized she just needed to reframe the way she looked at her relationship with Zane. Because of the child, they would always be a part of each other's lives, just in a nontraditional way.

As she packed up her toiletries and stowed them in the restaurant's office, she made a mental note to include Café St. Germaine in the acknowledgments. They had served as a handy home base today, and a cool reprieve from the summer heat.

Water bottle in hand and feeling refreshed, Lucy was going over her speech in her head as she made her way to the stage. She was on in five minutes and the fireworks extravaganza was scheduled to begin immediately after she finished.

The band was playing a medley of Fourth of July classics that sounded a little funky played on electric guitars, but the crowd seemed to be eating it up. That was all that mattered. Things didn't always have to be perfect—or her mind's-eye version of perfect. Different could be the spice that made life interesting.

As she waited by the side of the stage for the band to finish, she took out her phone to write that thought down in her notepad for the times she needed a gentle reminder.

"Excuse me," said a deep voice that made her heart compress and nearly explode. "Have I missed the fireworks?"

Zane was standing in front of her. Without thinking about it or asking his permission, she threw herself into his arms.

"Oh, my gosh, you're home! Why didn't you tell me you were coming home?"

"You didn't ask."

And just like that all the weirdness that had been between them melted away. Lucy could finally breathe. She hadn't realized she hadn't been able to breathe the entire time he had been gone—the entire time they hadn't talked. But standing here breathing the same air that he was breathing, she felt alive again.

"I'm so glad to see you. When did you get in?"

"About five minutes ago. Parking around here is hell. Do you know the name of the person who organizes this event? I want to file a complaint."

The lopsided smile that overtook his face was the most beautiful sight she had seen in ages. It took everything she had, every ounce of restraint, to keep from throwing her arms around his neck and kissing him. She took a physical step back as she reminded herself that she couldn't do that.

Don't mess things up.

Things were going to be okay as long as she remembered the boundaries.

"So you drove back to Celebration from Ocala today?"

"I did."

It was a Tuesday. The Sullivans had probably given him the day off, but it was curious that he hadn't stayed at the ranch. Surely, with their penchant for parties, the Sullivans would have a Fourth of July celebration that would make this one look like a rinky-dink outfit.

"When do you have to go back?"

He studied her for a moment and she wished she could read his thoughts.

"That depends. I had some business to take care of here in town."

Oh. It stood to reason. He was probably preparing to move out of the Bridgemont house. He'd need to clear out to make way for the new general manager.

"Hey, I got your message about my dad calling you. Thanks for looking out for me and not giving him my number. But there's a funny story that goes along with that. He has actually purchased the Old Wickham Road property. You know, my mom's family's old ranch. He wants to sell it to Ian and me for one dollar."

Lucy's mouth dropped open. "Holy cow. Are you serious?"

Zane nodded, looking a little dazed.

"What are you going to do? Are you going to accept his offer?"

Zane shrugged. "I talked to my brother and he says he can cough up the fifty cents for his part. Nathaniel says it's no deal for any other price. He said it's the least he can do for us after being such a louse when we were growing up. I mean, it's our legacy—and I quit the job at Hidden Rock."

"What?"

He nodded. "It was a great opportunity—for someone. But it wasn't for me. I'm back, but we can talk about that later. I need to mull over Nathaniel's offer…"

It sounded like Zane wanted her opinion on whether he was doing the right thing or not.

Of course, he would never come right out and ask her for advice. That was the way they'd always done things; he'd never had to ask because she had always offered an opinion, with the understanding that he could take it or leave it.

"Do you want to know what I think?" she asked.

He nodded, which was more than he used to do in the past. She was half expecting a snarky quip. But the band was finishing up and she was due to go up on stage—and Zane was here. He was *here and everything was going to be okay*. Her heart was so full she knew she needed to get herself together before she got up on stage in front of the entire town.

Her favorite song, "Somethin' Stupid," started

playing in her head. She looked at Zane and pushed the internal mute button on the soundtrack to her life.

She was just starting to ascend the stairs to the bandstand as the lead singer started introducing her. Or she thought he was introducing her. He was supposed to be introducing her. But instead he said, "If I could have everybody's attention, we have a special treat for you all tonight before we unleash the fireworks."

Special treat? She'd always wanted to be somebody's *special treat*, but not in this context. Her speech wasn't exactly a special treat, either. The guy had sort of oversold it.

Before she could take the microphone, Zane had slipped in behind her and took it in hand.

"Happy Fourth of July, everyone! It's good to be back in town. I'm Zane Phillips, for those of you who don't know me."

What in the—

Lucy looked around like she might find the answer to what was going on somewhere behind her, but, of course, she didn't. So she just let Zane do whatever it was that he was doing.

"Sometimes it takes getting exactly what you *think* you want to help you realize what's really important in life," he said.

He was looking right at Lucy.

Oh, my—

Was she hearing him right?

"Having your family around you is important. So

is the love of a good woman. Lucy, will you please come here?"

She hadn't realized it until now, but she had been backing up, small step by small step, until she was hiding safely in the shadows. Zane turned around and took her hand. "Come here, please? I have something important to say."

Most of her body was numb. The only thing she could feel was her pounding heart and her hopes rising ever so slightly with every step she took toward Zane.

"I have put you through hell the last couple of months. It's taken me a while to figure out what was in my heart, but while I've been away the only thing that I think of every morning when I wake up is you. You're the first thing on my mind in the morning and the last thing on my mind before I go to sleep. *It's you, Lucy. It's always been you. I love you.*"

Zane pulled something from the front pocket of his jeans and dropped to one knee. That was when she realized he was holding a small black box. "It took almost losing you to realize that I've always loved you. Will you make me the happiest man in the world and be my wife?"

Everyone in Central Park cheered. Through her tears, Lucy managed to choke out, "Yes."

As Zane pulled her into his arms and kissed her as if he was making up for all the hours they had been apart, the fireworks started behind them.

Zane grabbed her hand and led her off the bandstand to a picnic blanket, where he had a real ice bucket holding a bottle of champagne and Dorothy's crystal glasses waiting.

"I know they're not champagne glasses," he said. "I hope that's okay."

"They couldn't be more perfect."

As they toasted their love, the tears in her eyes made the crystal glasses gleam. Or maybe it was the sparkle of the diamond ring that Zane had put on her finger.

Zane loved her. He loved her.

Cinderella and Prince Charming had nothing on the two of them.

But the one thing she and Cinderella did have in common was that they both had found there happily-ever-after. Only, Lucy had Zane, who in real life was so much better than the Prince Charming in her mind that she had tried to turn him into.

Zane was the only man she'd ever loved. The only man she ever would love. His realizing that he loved her, too, was so worth the wait.

* * * * *

*And don't miss Jude and Juliette's
second chance at love in
THE COWBOY WHO GOT AWAY
the next book in the* CELEBRATION, TX
miniseries, available October 2017!

*And catch up with Ethan and Chelsea in
THE COWBOY'S RUNAWAY BRIDE
available now wherever Harlequin Special Edition
books and ebooks are sold!*

Katrina Bailey's life is at a crossroads, so when arrogant—but sexy—Bowie Callahan asks for her help caring for his newly discovered half brother, she accepts, never expecting it to turn into something more...

Read on for a sneak peek at SERENITY HARBOR, the next book in the HAVEN POINT series by New York Times bestselling author RaeAnne Thayne available July 2017!

CHAPTER ONE

"THAT'S HIM AT your six o'clock, over by the tomatoes. Brown hair, blue eyes, ripped. Don't look. Isn't he *gorgeous*?"

Katrina Bailey barely restrained from rolling her eyes at her best friend. "How am I supposed to know that if you won't let me even sneak a peek at the man?" she asked Samantha Fremont.

Sam shrugged with another sidelong look in the man's direction. "Okay. You can look. Just make it subtle."

Mere months ago, all vital details about her best friend's latest crush might have been the most fascinating thing the two of them talked about all week. Right now, she found it tough to work up much interest in one more man in a long string of them, especially with everything else she had spinning in her life right now.

She wanted to ignore Sam's request and continue on with shopping for the things they needed to take to Wynona's shower—but friends didn't blow off their friends' obsessions. She loved Sam and had missed hanging out with her over the last nine months. It made her sad that their interests appeared to have diverged so dramatically, but it wouldn't hurt her to act like she cared about the cute newcomer to Haven Point.

Donning her best ninja spy skills—honed from years of doing this very thing, checking out hot guys without them noticing—she pretended to reach up to grab a can of peas off the shelf. She studied the label intently, all while shifting her gaze toward the other end of the aisle.

About ten feet away, she spotted two men. Considering she knew Darwin Twitchell well—and he was close to eighty years old and cranky as a badger with gout—the other guy had to be Bowie Callahan, the new director of research and development at the Caine Tech facility in town.

Years of habit couldn't be overcome by sheer force of will. That was the only reason her stomach muscles seemed to shiver and her toes curled against the leather of her sandals. Or so she told herself, anyway.

Okay. She got it. Sam was totally right. The man was indeed great-looking: tall, lean, tanned, with sculpted features and brown hair streaked with the sort of blond highlights that didn't come from a salon but from spending time outside.

Under other circumstances, she might have wanted to do more than look. In a different life, perhaps she would have made her way to his end of the aisle, pretended to fumble with an item on the shelf, then dropped it right at his feet so they could "meet" while they both reached to pick it up.

She used to be such an idiot.

The old Katrina might not have been able to look away from such a gorgeous male specimen. But when he aimed a ferocious scowl downward, she shifted her gaze to find him frowning at a boy who looked to be about five or six, trying his best to put a box of sugary cereal into their cart and growing visibly upset when Bowie Callahan kept taking it out and putting it back on the shelf.

Katrina frowned. "You didn't say he had a kid. I thought you had a strict rule. No divorced dads."

"He doesn't have a kid!" Sam exclaimed.

"Then who's the little kid currently winding up for what looks like a world-class tantrum at his feet?"

Ignoring her own stricture about not staring, Sam whirled around. Her eyes widened with confusion. "I have no idea! I heard it straight from Eliza Caine that he's not married and doesn't have a family. He never said anything to me about a kid when I met him at a party at Snow Angel Cove or the other two times I've bumped into him around town this spring. I haven't seen him around for a few weeks. Maybe he has family visiting. Or maybe he's babysitting or something."

That was so patently ridiculous, Katrina had to bite her tongue. Really? Did Sam honestly believe the new director of research and development at Caine

Tech would be offering babysitting services—in the middle of the day and on a Monday, no less?

She sincerely adored Samantha for a million different reasons, but sometimes her friend saw what she wanted to see.

This latest example of how their paths had diverged in recent months made her a little sad. Until a year ago, she and Sam had been—as her mom would say—two peas of the same pod. They shared the same taste in music, movies, clothes. They could spend hours poring over celebrity and fashion magazines, dishing about the latest gossip, shopping for bargains at thrift stores and yard sales.

And men. She didn't even want to think about how many hours of her life she had wasted with Sam, talking about whichever guy they were most interested in that day.

Samantha had been her best friend since they found each other in junior high in that mysterious way like discovered like.

She still loved her dearly. Sam was kind and generous and funny, but Katrina's own priorities had shifted. After the events of the last year, Katrina was beginning to realize she barely resembled the somewhat shallow, flighty girl she had been before she grabbed her passport and hopped on a plane with Carter Ross.

That was a good thing, she supposed, but she felt a little pang of fear that while on the path to gaining a little maturity, she might end up losing her best friend.

"Babysitting. I suppose it's possible," she said in a noncommittal voice. If so, the guy was really lousy at it. The boy's face had reddened, and tears had started streaming down his features. By all appearances, he was approaching a meltdown, and Bowie Callahan's scowl had shifted to a look of helpless frustration.

"If you want, I can introduce you," Sam said, apparently oblivious to the drama.

Katrina purposely pushed their cart forward, in the opposite direction. "You know, it doesn't look like a good time. I'm sure I'll have a chance to meet him later. I'll be in Haven Point for a month. Between Wyn's wedding and Lake Haven Days, there should be plenty of time to socialize with our newest resident."

"Are you sure?" Sam asked, disappointment clouding her gaze.

"Yeah. Let's just finish shopping so I have time to go home and change before the shower."

Not that her mother's house really felt like home anymore. Yet another radical change in the last nine months.

"I guess you're right," Sam said, after another surreptitious look over Katrina's shoulder. "We waited too long, anyway. Looks like he's moved to another aisle."

They found the items they needed and moved to the next aisle as well, but didn't bump into Bowie again. Maybe he had taken the boy, whoever he was, out of the store so he could cope with his meltdown in private.

They were nearly finished shopping when Sam's phone rang with the ominous tone she used to identify her mother.

She pulled the device out of her purse and glared at it. "I wish I dared to ignore her, but if I do, I'll hear about it for a week."

That was nothing, she thought. If Katrina ignored *her* mother's calls while she was in town for Wyn's wedding, Charlene would probably mount a search and rescue, which was kind of funny when she thought about it. Charlene hadn't been nearly as smothering when Kat had been living halfway around the world in primitive conditions for the last nine months. But if she dared show up late for dinner, sheer panic ensued.

"I'm at the grocery store with Kat," Samantha said, a crackly layer of irritation in her voice. "I texted you that's where I would be."

Her mother responded something Katrina couldn't hear, which made Sam roll her eyes. To others, Linda Fremont could be demanding and cranky, quick to criticize. Oddly, she had always treated Katrina with tolerance and even a measure of kindness.

"Do you absolutely need it tonight?" Samantha asked, pausing a moment to listen to her mother's answer with obvious impatience written all over her features. "Fine. Yes. I can run over. I only wish you had mentioned this earlier, when I was just hanging around for three hours doing nothing, waiting for someone to show up at the shop. I'll grab it."

She shut off her phone and shoved it back into her little dangly Coach purse that she'd bought for a steal at the Salvation Army in Boise. "I need to stop in next door at the drugstore to pick up one of my mom's prescriptions. Sorry. I know we're in a rush."

"No problem. I'll finish the shopping and check out, then we can meet each other at your car when we're done."

"Hey, I just had a great idea," Sam exclaimed. "After the shower tonight, we should totally head up to Shelter Springs and grab a drink at the Painted Moose!"

Katrina tried not to groan. The last thing she wanted to do amid her lingering jet lag was visit the local bar scene, listening to the same songs, flirting with the same losers, trying to laugh at their same old, tired jokes.

"Let's play it by ear. We might be having so much fun at the shower that we won't want to leave. Plus it's Monday night, and I doubt there will be much going on at the PM."

She didn't have the heart to tell Sam she wasn't the same girl who loved nothing more than dancing with a bunch of half-drunk cowboys—or that she had a feeling she would never be that girl again. Priorities had a way of shifting when a person wasn't looking.

Sam stuck her bottom lip out in an exaggerated

pout. "Don't be such a party pooper! We've only got a month together, and I've missed you *so much*!"

Great. Like she needed more guilt in her life.

"Let's play it by ear. Go grab your mom's prescription, I'll check out and we'll head over to Julia's place. We can figure out our after-party plans, well, after the party."

She could tell by Sam's pout that she would have a hard time escaping a late night with her. Maybe she could talk her into just hanging out by the lakeshore and talking.

"Okay. I guess we'd better hurry if we want to have time to make our salad."

Sam hurried toward the front doors, and Katrina turned back to her list. Only the items from the vegetable aisle, then she would be done. She headed in that direction and spotted a flustered Bowie Callahan trying to keep the boy with him from eating grapes from the display.

"Stop it, Milo. I told you, you can eat as many as you want *after* we buy them."

This only seemed to make the boy more frustrated. She could see by his behavior and his repetitive mannerisms that he quite possibly had some sort of developmental issues. Autism, she would guess at a glance—though that could be a gross generalization, and she was not an expert, anyway.

Whatever the case, Callahan seemed wholly unprepared to deal with it. He hadn't taken the boy out of the store, obviously, to give him a break from the overstimulation. In fact, things seemed to have progressed from bad to worse.

Milo—cute name—reached for another grape despite the warning, and Bowie grabbed his hand and sternly looked down into his face. "I said, stop it. We'll have grapes after we pay for them."

The boy didn't like that. He wrenched his hand away and threw himself to the ground. "No! No! No!" he chanted.

"That's enough," Bowie Callahan snapped, loudly enough that other shoppers turned around to stare, which made the man flush.

She could see Milo was gearing up for a nuclear meltdown—and while she reminded herself it was none of her business, she couldn't escape a certain sense of professional obligation to step in.

She wanted to ignore it, to turn into the next aisle, finish her shopping and escape the store as quickly as she could. She could come up with a dozen excuses about why that was the best course of action. Samantha would be waiting for her. She didn't know the man or his frustrated kid. She had plenty of troubles of her own to worry about.

None of that held much weight when compared with the sight of a child, who clearly had some special needs, in great distress—and an adult who just as clearly didn't know what to do in the situation.

She felt an unexpected pang of sympathy for Bowie Callahan, probably because her mother had told her so many stories about how mortified Charlene would be when Katrina would have a seizure in a public place. All the staring, the pointing, the whispers.

The boy continued to chant "no" and began smacking his palm against his forehead in rhythm with each exclamation. A couple of older women she didn't know—tourists, probably—looked askance at the boy, and one muttered something to the other about how some children needed a swat on the behind.

She wanted to tell the old biddies to mind their own business but held her tongue, since she was about to ignore her own advice.

After another minute passed, when Bowie Callahan did nothing but gaze down at the boy with helpless frustration, Katrina knew she had to act. What other choice did she have? She pushed her cart closer. The man briefly met her gaze with a wariness that she chose to ignore. Instead, she plopped onto the ground next to the distressed boy.

In her experience with children of all ages and abilities, they reacted better to someone willing to lower to their level. She wasn't sure if he even noticed she was there, since he didn't stop chanting or smacking his palm against his head.

"Hi there." She spoke in a calm, conversational tone, as if she was chatting with one of her friends at Wynona's shower later in the evening. "What's your name?"

Milo—whose name she knew perfectly well from

hearing Bowie use it—barely took a breath. "No! No! No! No!"

"Mine is Katrina," she went on. "Some people call me Kat. You know. Kitty-cat. Meow. Meow."

His voice hitched a little, and he lowered his hand but continued chanting, though he didn't sound quite as distressed. "No. No. No."

"Let me guess," she said. "Is your name Batman?"

He frowned. "No. No. No."

"Is it… Anakin Skywalker?"

She picked the name, assuming by his Star Wars T-shirt it would be familiar to him. He shook his head. "No."

"What about Harry Potter?"

This time, he looked intrigued at the question, or perhaps at her stupidity. He shook his head.

"How about Milo?"

Big blue eyes widened with shock. "No," he said, though his tone gave the word the opposite meaning.

"Milo. Hi there. I like your name. I've never met anybody named Milo. Do you know anybody else named Kat?"

He shook his head.

"Neither do I," she admitted "But I have a cat. Her name is Marshmallow, because she's all white. Do you like marshmallows? The kind you eat, I mean."

He nodded and she smiled. "I do, too. Especially in hot cocoa."

He pantomimed petting a cat and pointed at her.

"You'd like to pet her? She would like that. She

lives with my mom now and loves to have anyone pay attention to her. Do you have a cat or a dog, Milo?"

The boy's forehead furrowed, and he shook his head, glaring up at the man beside him, who looked stonily down at both of them.

Apparently that was a touchy subject.

Did the boy talk? She had heard him say only "no" so far. It wasn't uncommon for children on the autism spectrum and with other developmental delays to have much better receptive language skills than expressive skill, and he obviously understood and could get his response across fairly well without words.

"I see lots of delicious things in your cart— including cherries. Those are my favorite. Yum. I must have missed those. Where did you find them?"

He pointed to another area of the produce section, where a gorgeous display of cherries gleamed under the fluorescent lights.

She pretended she didn't see them. Though the boy's tantrum had been averted for now, she didn't think it would hurt anything if she distracted him a little longer. "Do you think you could show me?"

It was a technique she frequently employed with her students who might be struggling, whether that was socially, emotionally or academically. She found that if she enlisted their help—either to assist her or to help out another student—they could often be distracted enough that they forgot whatever had upset them.

Milo craned his neck to look up at Bowie Callahan for permission. The man looked down at both of them, a baffled look on his features, but after a moment he shrugged and reached a hand down to help her off the floor.

She didn't need assistance, but it would probably seem rude to ignore him. She placed her hand in his and found it warm and solid and much more calloused than a computer nerd should have. She tried not to pay attention to the little shock of electricity between them or the tug at her nerves.

"Thanks," she mumbled, looking quickly away as she followed the boy, who, she was happy to notice, seemed to have completely forgotten his frustration.

Don't miss SERENITY HARBOR
by RaeAnne Thayne
available wherever HQN books
and ebooks are sold!

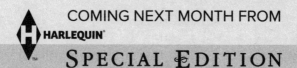

COMING NEXT MONTH FROM

HARLEQUIN®

SPECIAL EDITION

Available July 18, 2017

#2563 MOMMY AND THE MAVERICK
Montana Mavericks: The Great Family Roundup
by Meg Maxwell
Billionaire businessman Autry Jones swore off single mothers after enduring the pain of losing both the woman he loved *and* her child when she dumped him. That is, until he meets widowed mother of three Marissa Jones, who changes his mind—and his life—in three weeks.

#2564 DO YOU TAKE THIS COWBOY?
Thunder Mountain Brotherhood • by Vicki Lewis Thompson
Recently returned to Wyoming from New Zealand, Austin Teague is determined to find a wife and settle down. But he manages to fall hard for the fiercely independent Drew Martinelli, the one woman who's dead set against getting married.

#2565 HOW TO TRAIN A COWBOY
Texas Rescue • by Caro Carson
Benjamin Graham is a former marine, not a cowboy. So when he gets a job as a ranch hand, he has a lot to learn. Luckily, Emily Davis is willing to teach him everything he needs to know. But as the attraction between them grows, Graham and Emily will both have to face their pasts and learn to embrace the future.

#2566 VEGAS WEDDING, WEAVER BRIDE
Return to the Double C • by Allison Leigh
It looks like Penny Garner and Quinn Templeton had a Vegas wedding when they wake up in bed together with rings and a marriage certificate. While they put off a divorce to determine if she's pregnant, can Quinn convince Penny to leave her old heartbreak in the past and become his Weaver bride?

#2567 THE RANCHER'S UNEXPECTED FAMILY
The Cedar River Cowboys • by Helen Lacey
Helping Cole Quartermaine reconnect with his daughter was all Ash McCune intended to do. Falling for the sexy single dad was not part of the plan. But plans, she quickly discovers, have a way of changing!

#2568 AWOL BRIDE
Camden Family Secrets • by Victoria Pade
After a car accident leaves runaway bride Maicy Clark unconscious, she's rescued by the last man on earth she ever wanted to see again: Conor Madison, her high school sweetheart, who rejected her eighteen years ago. And if that isn't bad enough, she's stranded in a log cabin with him, in the middle of a raging blizzard, with nothing to do but remember just how good they were together.

_____

HSECNM0717

SPECIAL EXCERPT FROM

H HARLEQUIN®

SPECIAL EDITION

*Billionaire businessman Autry Jones swore off single
mothers—until he meets widowed mom of three
Marissa Jones just weeks before he's supposed to leave
for a job in Paris...*

Read on for a sneak preview of
MOMMY AND THE MAVERICK
by Meg Maxwell, *the second book in the*
*MONTANA MAVERICKS: THE GREAT FAMILY
ROUNDUP continuity.*

"Right. We shook on being friends. But..." She paused and
dropped down onto the love seat across from the fireplace.

"But things feel more than friendly between us," he finished
for her. "There was that kiss, for one. And the fact that every
time I see you I want to kiss you again."

"Ditto. See the problem?"

He smiled and sat down beside her. "Marissa, why did you
come here? To tell me that doing the competition with Abby is
a bad idea? That she's going to get too attached to me?"

"Yup."

"Except you didn't say that."

"Because I don't want to take it from her. I want her to be
excited about the competition. To not lose out on something
when she's been dealt a hard blow in life so young. But yeah, I
am worried she's going to get too attached. All three girls. But
especially Abby."

"Abby knows I'm leaving for Paris at the end of August.
That's a given. Goodbye is already in the air, Marissa. We're
not fooling anyone."

"Why do I keep fighting it, then?" she asked. "Why do I have to keep reminding myself that feeling the way I do about you is only going to—"

"Make you feel like crap when I go? I know. I've had that same talk with myself fifty times. I wasn't expecting to meet you, Marissa. Or want you so damned bad every time I see you."

It wasn't just about sex, but he wasn't putting that out there. If she kept it to sexual attraction, surface stuff, maybe he'd believe it. Then he could enjoy his time with Marissa and go in a couple weeks without much strain in his chest.

"So what do we do?" she asked. "Give in to this or be smart and stay nice and platonic?"

He reached for her hand. "I don't know."

"Your hair's still damp," she said. "I can smell your shampoo. And your soap."

He leaned closer and kissed her, his hands slipping around her shoulders, down her back, drawing her to him. He felt her stiffen for a second and then relax. "I don't want to just be friends, Marissa. I want you."

She kissed him back, her hands in his hair, and he could feel her breasts against his chest. He sucked in a breath, overwhelmed by desire, by need. "You're sure?" he asked, pulling back a bit to look at her, directly into her beautiful dark brown eyes.

"No, I'm not sure," she whispered. "I just know that I want you, too."

Don't miss
MOMMY AND THE MAVERICK by Meg Maxwell,
available August 2017 wherever
Harlequin® Special Edition books and ebooks are sold.

www.Harlequin.com

Reward the book lover in you!

Earn points from all your Harlequin book purchases from wherever you shop.

Turn your points into *FREE BOOKS* of your choice
OR
EXCLUSIVE GIFTS from your favorite authors or series.

Join for FREE today at
www.HarlequinMyRewards.com.

Harlequin My Rewards is a free program (no fees) without any commitments or obligations.

MYR17

SILHOUETTE Romance®

presents a brand-new title in

CAROL GRACE'S

heartwarming miniseries

Fairy Tale Brides

Cinderellie!

(Silhouette Romance #1775)
Available July 2005
at your favorite retail outlet.

Handsome venture capitalist Jack Martin had the
power to make Ellie Branson's dreams come true.
But could a man who wasn't looking for lasting
love really be her Prince Charming?

Also look for the next Fairy Tale Brides romance:

His Sleeping Beauty

(Silhouette Romance #1792, November 2005)

eHARLEQUIN.com

The Ultimate Destination for Women's Fiction

For FREE online reading, visit
www.eHarlequin.com now and enjoy:

Online Reads
Read **Daily** and **Weekly** chapters from
our Internet-exclusive stories by your
favorite authors.

Interactive Novels
Cast your vote to help decide how these
stories unfold...then stay tuned!

Quick Reads
For shorter romantic reads, try our
collection of Poems, Toasts, & More!

Online Read Library
Miss one of our online reads?
Come here to catch up!

Reading Groups
Discuss, share and rave with other
community members!

**For great reading online,
visit www.eHarlequin.com today!**

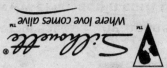

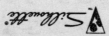

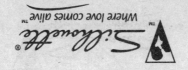